Better Press Pause

Mereo Books

2nd Floor, 6-8 Dyer Street, Cirencester, Gloucestershire, GL7 2PF
An imprint of Memoirs Books. www.mereobooks.com
and www.memoirsbooks.co.uk

Better Press Pause
ISBN: 978-1-86151-862-0

First published in Great Britain in 2024
by Mereo Books, an imprint of Memoirs Books.

The address for Memoirs Books can be
found at www.mereobooks.com

Mereo Books Ltd. Reg. No. 12157152

Typeset in 12/19pt Garamond
by Wiltshire Associates.
Printed and bound in Great Britain

Struggling to manage relations with parents,
a playground bully and schoolboy crushes, Ben stumbles upon
a device with strange powers that might just help.

Better Press Pause

Simon Ireland

CHAPTER 1

'Benji, have you finished today's Maths problems yet?'

Ben glanced up from his laptop screen and sighed in frustration. It was bad enough having to spend what seemed a lifetime on the world's most boring assignment without being checked up on at regular intervals. And as for his pet name being used, well that simply added insult to injury. Still, bitter experience had taught him that nothing could dissuade his mother from calling him that, so he simply gritted his teeth, pushed a sweaty strand of fair hair away from his eyes and trotted out his stock answer.

'Almost there, Mum, just a couple of questions to go.'

Whatever the task, this usually did the trick. Squinting through the kitchen window, he could see his mother giving him the thumbs up before returning to the task of hosing down the family Labrador, Molly.

Not for the first time, she – the dog that is – had rolled in something unspeakable in the nearby woods and on such a sweltering day the resulting pong was particularly pungent. *Pong... particularly... pungent...* Ben made a mental note to file away this example of alliteration so that he could impress his sarcastic English teacher – if he ever returned to class after this Covid lockdown.

Molly, meanwhile, shook herself dry on the patio, water droplets arcing and sparkling in the sunshine before landing on the laughing Mrs Wilson.

'Oh, Molly! I've had one shower already today, thank you VERY much. Now stay out here and get properly dry. You may like the aroma of Eau de Fox Poo but I certainly don't appreciate it inside the house.'

Picking up the hosepipe and wrapping it back round the outside tap, Ben's mum made her way back into the kitchen, where she bent over her son's shoulder to check his progress.

'Mmm, nice perfume.' Ben chuckled. 'Men are going to find you irresistible – not!'

As soon as the words passed his lips, Ben regretted them. It was only last year that his parents had split up, and his mother's confidence had been badly bruised. He longed for her to be her old happy self again, but as an average sport and computer games obsessed 11-year-old, he hardly felt qualified to give out relationship advice.

Mikey, his best friend, had recently informed him that

most "crusties" went on line these days to find a partner and advised that Ben's mum needed to get herself a "sick" profile ASAP. Unsurprisingly, Ben had yet to broach the subject and, to be honest, in his heart of hearts he still hoped that she could find a way to forgive his dad.

* * *

Two miles away, on the outskirts of town, the man in question was busy doing what he did best – absolutely nothing. Being furloughed had given Ben's dad the ideal opportunity to sort out his poky flat and, in particular, transform the spare bedroom into a welcoming sleepover space for his son. As usual, however, he was glued to his phone.

His sweaty fingers were switching from one betting site to another while he did his best to withstand the blizzard of special deals and new customer offers. Despite the fact that his spiralling gambling debts had led to the end of his marriage, he still told himself that he was just one big win away from salvation, one big win away from showing Ben that he wasn't a complete waste of space as a dad.

'When the fun stops, stop!' Not for the first time, he grimaced as the ridiculous message appeared on the screen. Almost bankrupting his family hadn't been 'fun'; having to beg friends for emergency loans hadn't been 'fun'; bringing his marriage to an end and saying goodbye to Margaret hadn't been 'fun'. But here he was again, just one or two clicks away from the same old nightmare repeating itself.

'Snap out of it!' he told himself and flung his phone onto the settee in frustration. He then stood up, stretched and promptly tripped over one of the many boxes he had yet to unpack. This one was crammed with audio leads, plugs and remote control handsets from long since discarded TVs, DVD players and stereo systems. He had been meaning to sift through the treasures in this electrical Aladdin's cave, but instead he stuffed the snaking contents back into the cardboard box and slid it under the corner cupboard.

'Out of sight, out of mind,' he muttered to himself before switching on the TV to catch the day's Downing Street briefing. 'Maybe I'll get round to having a proper clear out tomorrow – and maybe Ben will give me a hand, too. That is if we are still allowed to be in the same house, of course!'

*   *   *

In truth, several months of coronavirus restrictions had been more of a challenge for Ben's parents than the sparky eleven-year-old himself. Zoom lessons and the endless assignments had at least spared him most of a final term in the company of Nathan Bolt and his cronies, and the good weather had allowed him to work on his soccer skills in the garden. Molly was a nuisance, of course, but he generally assigned her the role of defender and imagined that when he waltzed past her to score, he was Harry Kane netting against Arsenal in a frenzied North London derby. Not that he could actually remember the last time Tottenham had won one of these contests.

And then there was the mobile phone that he had persuaded his mum to allow him on the grounds of safety. He was in regular contact with Mikey (even if they weren't meeting face to face that often) and they swapped assignment answers, jokes and gossip. Being the smallest boy in Year 6, Mikey had also been one of Nathan Bolt's regular victims and between them, he and Ben were determined to come up with a master plan that would see 'Nasty Nathan' well and truly given a taste of his own medicine before Senior School beckoned and they went their separate ways.

As St Peter's Primary had organised a farewell disco and awards evening for Year 6 at the end of the school year, Covid rules permitting, both Ben and Mikey had been imagining a glorious revenge which saw humiliation for the bullying Nathan and his henchmen and a suitably heroic triumph for themselves. The details of what would ACTUALLY happen were yet to be confirmed, but it gave Ben a warm feeling just thinking about Nathan's inevitable demise.

Of course, had he known exactly what fate did have in store for him, then instead of just experiencing a warm feeling, he would have been dancing round the garden with Molly and yelling 'In your face, Nathan Nobody!' at the top of his voice.

CHAPTER 2

As it was, the next morning found Ben trudging dutifully towards his dad's new flat. He was doing his best to follow his mum's advice and give older people a wide berth if they shuffled past with their face masks half on and half off. His dad had invited him over to help sort out what would be known as 'Ben's Den'; the deal was that afterwards he could order whatever food he wanted to be delivered.

It was another glorious day and despite the confusing tiered restrictions, Ben could see local residents trying to make the best of things as they emerged from temporary hibernation: cars were being cleaned, flowerbeds weeded and dogs walked. The nearer he got to the flat, though, the more down-at-heel the properties became in the nondescript north London suburb, and Ben soon found himself picking his way between discarded coffee cups and fast food packaging.

He was tempted to dribble a crushed Coke can along the pavement, but thought better of it, as he knew exactly what his mother would have said about such 'hooligan tendencies'. Instead, he bent down and picked it up carefully – along with two empty crisp packets and a half-eaten pasty which a delivery driver had obviously tossed out of his van window.

Feeling rather pleased with himself for showing such a sense of civic duty, Ben started to walk towards an upturned litter bin which lay at the corner of his dad's road. He hadn't taken more than three or four steps when a vinegary female voice cut through the morning air.

'Don't you dare drop your litter in this street, you young rascal. I know your type only too well!'

'But I was just about to...' Ben began to explain before another tirade stopped him in his tracks.

'Just about to add to the filth that's already ruining this area, you mean. If I've complained to the council once, I've complained a hundred times and yet nothing gets done – EVER!'

And with that the sharp-featured, grey-haired woman who was leaning over her garden hedge disappeared into her flat and slammed the front door.

'Well, I'm glad I don't live next door to a dragon like you!' Ben muttered to himself. Still chuntering away, he wrestled the bin into submission and shoved the litter inside. Wiping his hands on the sides of his jeans, he approached the block which contained Flat 28, his dad's new home.

He gulped. It was the very next building. Ben might not have lived next to a grey-haired dragon, but his dad most certainly did.

* * *

Discretion being the better part of valour, as his Form Tutor liked to say, not that Ben entirely understood the meaning of the phrase, the eleven-year-old scuttled along beneath the level of the hedge and escaped into his dad's driveway. As the door was lying half open, he plunged straight in without knocking.

Safely inside, he breathed a sigh of relief.

'Hey, where's the fire?' his dad said with a laugh. 'Good to see you, buddy.'

Ben's father, Steve Wilson, was like a bigger version of his son. Despite all that life had thrown at him recently, the car salesman could still summon an impish smile and his fair hair remained thick and unruly. He was wearing cargo pants, trainers and his favourite David Bowie T-shirt and holding a burnt piece of toast plastered in chocolate spread. Ben immediately thought back to the way his mother had complained bitterly about his dad's sloppy dress sense and how he never seemed to 'grow up and take responsibility'. Still, Ben was secretly rather proud that HIS dad seemed so much younger and cooler than those of his classmates.

'Sorry,' he gasped, 'I didn't mean to startle you. I just...'

'...Wanted to get away from Mrs Snyde, my lovely new next door neighbour.' Steve sighed. 'I thought I heard her dulcet tones a moment ago. What's the old bag moaning about this time?'

'Oh, nothing important really, just the rubbish in the road.'

'Well, it is a bit of a rubbish area, come to think of it!'

Ben groaned in mock pain and grinned at his father. As well as their colouring, the two shared the same love of puns and bad jokes.

'Good one, Dad. I suppose that's what you call a "throwaway" remark!'

Knowing when he was beaten, Ben's dad smiled ruefully and made his way into what passed for the kitchen in his modest new accommodation. He switched on the radio and opened the fridge door. Whistling along tunelessly to Lewis Capaldi, he surveyed the rather pathetic contents and promptly closed it again.

'I've got some Coke, Ben, but that's about it. Look, why

don't we do some sorting out and then I'll get you that takeaway I promised.'

'Ok,' Ben replied. Looking around the lounge, he spotted a box of electrical odds and ends poking out from beneath the corner cupboard. He wandered over and pulled it out. Goodness only knows why his Dad had kept all this stuff. After all, how many remote controls, for example, did one man need?

He picked up what appeared to be the least old and battered device and was immediately struck by its iconic Star Wars logo and the VHS cassette it lay next to. Then he remembered his dad coming across a collector's item on eBay and spending more than he should have done on an 'interactive board game' from 1995. Steve Wilson's passion for Star Wars rarities had naturally cooled since his gambling debts had mounted, but Ben couldn't help smiling as he remembered the clunky cassette being inserted into an even clunkier video player and the delight with which his dad had demonstrated how people used to amuse themselves in the Dark Ages. The remote control allowed the player to access certain extra features and pause the game at strategic moments.

Keeping hold of the remote, he shoved the box back under the cupboard, letting his imagination run riot for a moment. Then he slipped the device into his pocket and adopted the stance of an American cop ready to draw his gun on an escaped criminal.

'Freeze, sucker, or I'll...'

At that point Ben's fantasy was rudely interrupted by a deafening blast of David Bowie's "Heroes" and his dad yelling, 'Hey, Ben, this is more like it! It's the Thin White Duke's best, if you ask me.'

But within seconds there was a pounding on the front door, followed by a shrill shriek of 'Turn that racket off!' and moments later Mrs Snyde appeared at the window, shaking her bony fist.

Steve turned the volume down and went to try and pacify his neighbour. As he did his best to apologise, he was unaware that his son was hovering behind him: Ben was imagining that he could mute the barrage of criticism coming his Dad's way by pointing the remote control at Mrs Snyde and pressing the appropriate button.

Which, to Ben's utter amazement, was exactly what happened.

CHAPTER 3

Ben's heart was racing as he peered round his dad's cargo pants at the angry face of Mrs Snyde. Her lips were moving, but he couldn't hear a sound. The strange thing was that his dad seemed to be carrying on the conversation and reacting to the accusations, while all that Ben could hear was the sound of his own breathing.

Swallowing nervously, he pressed the mute button again. Once again he was swamped by the tidal wave of Mrs Snyde's continued vitriol.

Hmm… so it appeared that while he was holding the remote control, then he alone benefited from its powers. Was that the deal? To double check, he sought out the Pause button, took a deep breath and let his thumb work its magic again.

To his amazement, time seemed to stand still. There was Mrs Snyde, wild-eyed and frozen in mid-rant; there was his dad, captured with his hands out in mid-apology. Looking over their shoulders, Ben could see no cars driving past, no birds flying and no pedestrians shuffling past. The world had stopped – or Ben had stopped it.

The enormity of what was happening, or not happening, was almost too much to take in. Ben took a step or two back into the lounge and pressed Pause again. Instantly, the doorstep argument continued and the outside world resumed its reassuringly mundane patterns. He could feel his heart rate slowing as he slipped the remote control back into his pocket. But then he heard the front door slam, and before he knew it his father was slumped on the sofa, seething with frustration.

'Sorry about that, Ben, but she's been on my case ever since I moved in. And did you hear what she called me? Did you?'

Ben gulped then smiled weakly. 'I know, Dad, I couldn't believe my eyes... er... my ears, I mean,' he stuttered.

But he needn't have worried, Steve Wilson was too preoccupied with his own outrage to pick up on what could have been a rather revealing slip of the tongue.

* * *

Four hours and four large pieces of pepperoni pizza later, Ben was making his way home in unusually thoughtful fashion.

He could feel the remote control rubbing against his thigh, and his mind was full of the possibilities it represented. He was also desperate to reveal his discovery to Mikey and start planning Nathan's hour of reckoning in more detail.

'Wow,' he muttered to himself. ' If this little beauty works on Nathan like it did on Mrs Snyde then we could really have some fun!'

Just then he became aware of a familiar rumbling sound and looked up to see his diminutive friend skateboarding towards him along the deserted pavement. Mikey's freckled face was screwed up in concentration as he navigated his way past potential hazards such as cracks in the concrete and stubborn clumps of weeds.

'If it isn't Mikey the mighty atom!' called Ben. 'How's it going, my miniature mischief maker?'

One of the pair's ongoing games involved competing to see who could come up with the catchiest alliterative greeting; as yet, Mikey had still not got the better of his more creative pal.

'Um, brilliantly, Ben, my er, bosom buddy...'

'Steady on,' Ben chuckled. 'I know we're good mates, but let's not go too far!'

'Sorry,' Mikey said, looking rather shamefaced, 'I just couldn't think of anything else on the spur of the moment. If

I'd known we'd be bumping into each other I'd have come up with something better. Anyway, what have you been up to?'

Ben didn't reply immediately. Although he had been thrilled initially at the thought of sharing his amazing discovery with his friend, something told him that it was too soon, that letting Mikey into the secret and trying out the remote control all over the place would be like eating a box of chocolates all in one go. How much better it would be to take his time, to investigate just how reliable and effective the device was and THEN relish planning exactly how to put it to its best possible use, particularly in their ongoing war with Nathan Bolt.

'Oh, nothing too exciting,' he eventually replied. 'I've just been over at my dad's new place having some pizza and sorting out one of the rooms I might stay in.'

'Cool, I wondered why you were over in this bit of town. Slumming it, eh?'

Mikey lived in the area, as his parents, both from academic backgrounds, earned relatively little from their book reviewing and part-time tutoring. It had become a standing joke between the boys that Ben was somehow much posher but liked to mix with the 'common people' from time to time. The boys had once been driving to the shops with Ben's dad when the Pulp song of that name came on the radio, and it had planted the idea in Mikey's head.

'Yeah, yeah, that's it, I was just seeing how Artful Dodgers like you spend their time,' Ben joked.

'Well, guv'nor, there's nuffink like a bit of a scrap round the back of the old rub a dub dub to get the blood flowin', and then I'll be on the lookout for an old geezer or two to filch a quid from…'

And they were off, happily trading in their usual good-humoured banter and continuing to make frequent use of dialogue from last year's school play, 'Oliver'. Being Year 5 pupils then, they had missed out on the much-coveted lead roles but had proved ideal for playing members of Fagin's gang. Mikey, in fact, had almost stolen the show, being the smallest yet most confident of the performers, and Ben could still hear his mum after the dress rehearsal saying, 'Ooh, couldn't you just eat him up, he's so cute!'

Ben shuddered in mock horror at the recollection as the two boys continued on their happy way towards his house, where football with Molly in the garden would while away the rest of the afternoon.

Meanwhile, the remote control which was pressing against his leg reminded Ben that he would next have to find a suitable hiding place for the device that was hopefully going to turn Nathan's life upside down.

CHAPTER 4

So it was that after leaving Mikey to make his usual fuss of Molly in the back garden, Ben stole upstairs to the safety of his bedroom. Looking round at the familiar clutter of books, toys and trainers, he assessed his options. Under his bed? No, that was far too predictable. On the top of his wardrobe? No – what if his mother decided to embark on one of her infamous 'green cleans' now that she had jumped on the recycling wagon and seemed intent on saving the planet single-handedly?

And then he noticed the empty Chocolate Buttons tube left over from Christmas. He had kept it to store felt tips in, but they lay strewn all over his desk. Reaching inside his pocket, he carefully withdrew the remote control and slid it into the tube. Like a gun in a holster, it fitted snugly inside its new home, so Ben promptly added the tube to the other stationery items in his desk tidy and proceeded to rejoin his friend in the summer sunshine.

While the two friends practised their soccer skills and chased Molly round the apple tree, which provided a welcome patch of shade, Margaret Wilson sat staring at her computer screen. She had finished checking her email inbox and was trying to pluck up the courage to investigate a dating site one of the divorced mums at school had recommended. She and Ben's father had separated some nine months ago, and despite the heartache he had caused her over the years, she had to admit she missed having a man in her life. While she would always be grateful for the house and the comfortable early lifestyle his successes at the car dealership had brought the family, she couldn't see a future for them while gambling dominated Steve's thoughts. All things considered then, perhaps now was the right time to dip her toes in the shallow end of the dating scene by putting a profile together.

The question was, of course, how honest should she be? 'Harassed single mother, rapidly approaching forty, no immediate career prospects...' Well that wasn't going to float anyone's boat, was it? And what about a flattering photograph, if such a thing existed? She heaved a heartfelt sigh and looked up to see Ben and Mikey trying to outdo each other at 'keepy-uppy'.

What would her son feel about having a new man around? Although he had been joking the other day about the dog poo perfume putting men off, she knew how he idolised Steve and how hard he had been hit by his parents' split. Maybe she should wait a bit longer before posting anything on the 'Jacks4Jills' website...

* * *

Had Steve Wilson known what his wife was agonising over, he would probably have grinned at her usual indecision, then felt a sharp pang of guilt. After all, he was the root cause of all the personal and financial changes in their lives. But whether he himself could change was up for debate. It certainly didn't look like it, for he was once again fingering his credit card and scrolling through the odds being quoted on the first scorer in tonight's big game. He was doing this out of habit really, acting on autopilot after a boring afternoon of retiling his tiny bathroom while listening to the latest relaxation of restrictions on the radio. But it was proving a dangerously hard habit to break.

In normal times he would have been enjoying life at the car dealership, where his natural charm and sharp wits had enabled him to become one of their most successful salesmen. He loved the thrill of the chase and had an instinct for matching the right car to the right buyer. The banter with his co-workers had helped to make quieter days more tolerable, and there were also the prank calls to the rival dealership to plan and execute – as long as his boss wasn't around, of course.

But there was also the down side of having the means and the time to place the odd bet and insist to his mates that he was onto 'a sure thing'. And before long he had found himself locked into a cycle of frequent losses offset by the occasional wins that persuaded him that a change in fortune was just around the corner. Even worse, he became a practised liar who was able to assure his wife that particular bills had 'of course' been paid and the reason their joint account seemed somewhat depleted was down to a computer glitch in the bank's system.

In time, he had inevitably got caught out, tangled in his own web of increasingly complex half-truths and fabrications. He cringed with embarrassment at the memory of his wife's bank card being declined as she tried to pay for the weekly supermarket shop and the whispers and pointing fingers she had had to endure as she slunk out of the crowded store. Memories of the nuclear row that had followed still haunted him, not least Ben's tearful slamming and locking of his bedroom door when he couldn't take any more of his parents' screaming coming from the kitchen.

A trial separation had quickly ended when both parents saw the effect it was having on Ben's mental health at a key time in his school life; Year 6 brought enough pressures without domestic upheaval looming over him like the sword of Damocles. Tragically, Steve Wilson had then sabotaged any hopes of a permanent reconciliation by giving in to temptation for one final, catastrophic time....

* * *

This time it had been male pride as much as anything that got him into the deepest water yet as restrictions eased temporarily and businesses emerged hesitantly from their imposed suspension. A salesman from a rival dealership had been in the bookmakers Steve had begun to use on the other side of town in order to hide what he was up to from his long suffering wife. The usual banter had led to a challenge being laid down - a two part challenge, no less.

Darren Jackson boasted that customers would be gagging to take up his dealership's new summer offers and he would, of course, make a mint in commission. He had also been tipped off about a dead cert in the next flat race at Weatherby. So there was no way that Steve would (a) be earning more money in the next sales period or (b) be fleecing the bookies for a similarly 'nailed on' fortune. But if Steve was man enough, a grand for doing better in each half of the 'dealers' double' was on the table...

A possible two thousand pounds would normally have led to Ben's dad accepting the challenge like a shot, but even he had to stop and think this time. Family life and access to his son was hanging by a thread thanks to previous gambles, so surely he couldn't risk upsetting the fragile status quo. 'Down, down, deeper and down!' he promptly began to sing to himself ironically, plucking one of the three-chord wonder's finest from the giant juke box in his head. The play on words immediately made him think of Ben and a fresh wave of guilt swept over him; yet despite this he just knew that the two thousand temptations would inevitably win out and that wiping the smirk off Darren's face would be the dream bonus.

Equally inevitably, Steve was to lose out on both counts as a customer pulled out of buying a top of the range model at the last minute and his own 'sure thing' at York Races pulled up lame. He then had to endure Darren's jibes as well as the shame of not being able to settle an overdue plumber's bill which he had promised Ben's mum had been sorted. The one thing that did get 'sorted' was Steve getting his final marching orders from his wife and having to apologise to Ben for one last excruciating time.

Perhaps the poky rented flat next to the sour-faced Mrs Snyde was all he deserved at this point in proceedings for the elusive 'fun' that gambling adverts extolled had well and truly stopped.

CHAPTER 5

Having finished writing his own witch's spell in response to the latest English assignment, Ben stretched and pressed 'Save' on his laptop. Although he would not have admitted it, he had rather enjoyed the challenge of including ingredients that reflected 21st century life and picturing Nathan Bolt suffering the effects of the vile concoction. After all, helpings of toxic exhaust fumes and untreated sewage were the least the bully deserved.

> *'Smashed up bottles in the gutter,*
> *Vicious threats the Hoodies mutter;*
> *Junk food from a burger van,*
> *Sweeteners in a fizzing can!'*

Ben chanted the next verse of his spell and stamped about in time until his mum yelled in protest from the kitchen, where she was adding the finishing touches to her cheesy cottage pie. With his schoolwork now out of the way and feeling rather pleased with himself, Ben reached over to his desk tidy to check on the remote control that promised to transform the next few weeks in so many exciting ways. Unable to locate the cardboard Buttons tube at first, Ben upended the layered container and pored over the contents.

It was then that he felt a clammy sense of dread sweep over him.

The tube had gone!

* * *

Fifteen frantic minutes later, Ben had searched every nook and cranny in his room to no avail. He forced himself to think logically – if he himself hadn't moved the tube somewhere, then it could only have been his mother. Molly might have been sniffing about in the hope of locating a welcome snack, but there was no way the greedy Labrador would have made off with a tube that didn't actually contain food. So if it had been Mum, had she indeed embarked on one of her recycling purges or *Guardian*-inspired 'green cleans'? Ben hurried downstairs to check the designated bin by the back door, breathing in the appetising cheesy aroma as he rushed through the now empty kitchen.

'Tea won't be ready for another twenty minutes, Benji,' he heard his mother shout from the lounge.

'It's ok,' he replied, 'I'm just putting some old school project stuff in the recycling.'

'Well I AM impressed!' He heard her laugh as he shut the kitchen door and lifted the lid of the green bin. He carefully moved some of his mother's old gardening magazines to one side and breathed a huge sigh of relief; there, next to some squashed Amazon packaging, lay the Buttons tube, and inside he could make out the comfortingly squat shape of the remote control. What a stroke of luck that Mum had obviously just swept up the container alongside a load of other cardboard without stopping to look inside. But he couldn't afford another scare like this. As he crept back inside and up the stairs, he knew that his next hiding place would have to be a good deal more parent-proof.

Moments later, as he was looking around his bedroom, Ben's gaze fell upon the Stormtrooper helmet that his dad had attached to the wall. Of course – what more appropriate home could there be for his Star Wars related discovery?

A passion for Star Wars films was something else that father and son had in common, and Steve Wilson had made a good job of fixing the white mask to its sturdy mount. When Ben perched on the edge of his bed and reached up, he found that if he lifted the hollow mask up on its hinge, he could slip the remote control into the space behind and swing it back into position. Surely he could relax now, especially as his mother had absolutely zero interest in George Lucas's masterpiece...

* * *

Sadly, relaxation was soon far from Ben's mind. When he went back downstairs for his serving of cheesy cottage pie, he noticed that his mum had left her laptop on, so he nipped into the lounge while she was dishing up in the kitchen. The garish logo of the 'Jacks4Jills' dating site sprang into view when he tapped the screen. He gulped.

It appeared that his mum had found a possible match, and a Zoom call was in the process of being arranged with 'Guildford Guy'. Ben cringed with embarrassment, and then a fresh wave of panic swept over him. What was he going to do now? He felt like one of those entertainers spinning several plates at once and having to rush between them, but instead of plates, it was problems.

'Benji, come and get it while it's hot!'

His mother's voice forced him to abandon the laptop. He trudged into the kitchen, where Molly was already wagging her tail expectantly, for Ben was a safe bet when it came to under-the-table treats.

Sprinkling some cheese on as a final garnish, Ben's mum joked that she had 'grate expectations' of her signature dish. When her son failed to react to the pun, which she was secretly rather proud of, she frowned: it was highly unusual for him to turn down the chance of trading jokes. She was even more perplexed when, after toying with his food, he suddenly turned on her, tears in his eyes.

'Mum, you know that was a special game for dad and me. How could you be so mean!'

And with that Ben scraped back his chair and tore up the stairs to the sanctuary of his bedroom. Slamming and locking the door, he threw himself onto the bed and buried his face in his Tottenham Cockerel duvet. But only briefly, for while he felt bad about his dramatic over-reaction to his mum's attempt at humour, it had at least bought him some breathing space.

Now he had to come up with a plan of action - and quickly. For all he knew, his mum could be setting up the Zoom call with the gruesome-sounding Guildford Guy at this very minute. But then, when he had calmed down and begun to think more logically, he realised that she would be unlikely to risk Ben overhearing or interrupting the call, so she might well wait until he was out of the house. And she would also be finishing her meal off, so he had a few minutes to play with, at least.

So, what should he do in the meantime? His attention wandered round the room, from Lego model to Bowie poster to Tottenham scarf. He then considered the Stormtrooper helmet again. Of course, he could use the remote control to pause time and... and... yes, that was it, he could put a large sign behind his mum showing that she still loved his dad and leave it there just long enough for the Surrey sleazeball to get the message before unfreezing time and removing it before his mum realised something was wrong. Surely the call wouldn't lead to a date after that and he would have the breathing space to work out how to patch up his parents' relationship.

So Ben got to work immediately, daubing large felt-tip letters on the plain side of an old poster of Dele Alli. Now that the mercurial midfielder had left the club he didn't feel too bad about this and he hummed to himself as he wrote 'SHE STILL LOVES MY DAD!!!' in suitably large print.

He was just holding it up to his wardrobe mirror when he heard a tap at the door.

'Benji, I'm sorry about earlier. I was only trying to cheer you up, not depress you. I've kept your supper on a plate in the oven, so it should still be fine to eat whenever you feel like it. Just come back down when you feel better. I've got stuff to do on the laptop anyway.'

Alarm bells immediately rang in Ben's head; obviously he had underestimated his mother's desire to set the romantic ball rolling. He quickly folded his sign and put it behind the door ready for action. He mumbled that he would be down in a minute or two, and climbed up to retrieve the remote control.

Now he just had to hope that the Force would indeed be with him....

CHAPTER 6

A few moments later Ben was making his way downstairs as carefully as if each stair had been booby-trapped. The remote control was lodged securely in his back pocket and he was clutching his newly made sign in both hands so that there was no danger of the lettering getting smudged.

The lounge door was partially open and even in this moment of high tension Ben smiled to himself at the thought of his dad trotting out the old joke about a door not being a door when it was AJAR! Forcing himself to concentrate, he peered through the gap to be greeted by the sight of his Mum giggling girlishly as she played with her dark hair and leaned close to her laptop screen. Things were obviously progressing faster than anticipated. He would have to act quickly.

Propping the poster against the hall table, he took hold of the remote control, held his breath and pressed Pause. His mum promptly froze mid-flirt.

Ben looked for the ideal place to position his sign.

Having decided it would sit nicely on top of the bookcase immediately behind his mother's chair, he crept back to collect it, putting the remote on the bottom stair on the way.

And that was when he heard his mother giggle coquettishly once again.

A fresh wave of panic swept over Ben and he frantically assessed his options: either he could abort the mission and rush back upstairs, or he could try the remote again. Perhaps it had started playing up. 'Come on,' he told himself, 'you've come this far, you may as well see things through.' He quickly picked up the remote once more and pressed Pause. Straight away his mother's voice died mid-sentence.

Ben breathed a huge sigh of relief. He reckoned he needed both hands to get the poster into position without getting completely covered in felt tip, so he plonked the remote back down on the stair. And that was when he heard his mum's cringe inducing laughter resume...

Instinctively, Ben grabbed the remote for a third time and sought out the Pause button. The laughter stopped again. The penny finally dropped. The remote's functions only worked their magic for him when he was actually holding it.

He clamped his left hand on the poster and made his way into the lounge, where he just about managed to balance it so that it was leaning against the wall on top of the bookcase but directly behind his mother's head. Wiping his felt-tip-stained left hand on his jeans, while being careful to keep the remote firmly in his right, he retreated until he was lurking in the doorway and safely out of the picture, as it were. He then pressed Pause again. He promptly heard that same flirty laugh again, but it soon died away. His mother said a very bad word and fiddled with her keyboard.

'Guy, what is it? I seem to have lost you.'

Ben knew then that his plan had worked, at least in the short term. He pressed Pause again and retrieved the poster so that his mum would be none the wiser as to why her romantic journey had come to a shuddering halt. As he wriggled back through the doorway he half turned and pressed Pause for a final time. Creeping back up the stairs he could hear his mum muttering something about 'bloody men' and then the sound of her footsteps as she made her way into the kitchen for a consoling glass of Chardonnay.

Phew. Mission accomplished! Ben felt as if he was back to spinning plates once more, but at least he had stopped them crashing to the ground. He slid the poster under his bed, addressed the remote control and wagged a finger like one of his frustrated teachers.

'Now look here. Your behaviour is certainly not what it

should be at the moment and I don't want to be disappointed by you again. Is that clear?'

Reprimand complete, Ben swung the Stormtrooper mask away from the wall and carefully stowed the remote inside, just as his mother shouted from the kitchen that he really should be having his supper by now.

'Coming, mother dearest!' he yelled back and galloped down the stairs before jumping onto the hall rug and skidding along the parquet flooring like a skateboarder.

'Somebody's cheered up a bit, I'm glad to see,' his mother remarked. 'Wish I felt the same...' Her voice tailed off. She could hardly explain what had frustrated her so much without alerting Ben to her romantic aspirations. His recent outburst showed that he still harboured hopes of some sort of reconciliation, so perhaps it was just as well that Guildford Guy had done a disappearing act. For the time being, at least, he could be consigned to the back burner, like Ben's cheesy cottage pie.

* * *

It seemed, meanwhile, that the only recipe Steve Wilson was master of had disaster as its main ingredient. Across town he could be found attempting to address his latest financial woes; the postman seemed to deliver only brown envelopes and final demands these days. His usual dodge of putting off Peter to pay Paul had well and truly caught up with him and his only recourse, as ever, was to compare the odds and offers on the betting sites that had got him into this mess in the first place. How else was he going to come up with the money to settle his rent arrears and utility bills, let alone treat Ben to the new trainers he coveted?

He fanned out the bills on his coffee table like a fortune teller laying out Tarot cards: not that there was any doubt about what lay around the corner if he couldn't rustle up some funds in double quick time. And the endless succession of gambling firm adverts on his favourite radio station, TalkSport, didn't help either. The so-caring platitudes about customer safety being paramount and the importance of gambling 'responsibly' or 'taking time out' rang increasingly hollow as he reached across to switch off his battered radio in frustration.

As he did so he knocked over a pile of sports and music magazines. Swearing under his breath, he began to pick them up. Suddenly his attention was drawn to the TV schedules for next week's Premier League fixtures and on the facing page a strident 'Acca Alert' encouraging punters to build a series of bets and thereby 'win big'. Not that Steve needed much encouragement, of course. He was now feeling absolutely desperate, a man being sucked down into creditor quicksand with no one there to haul him out.

He studied the 'Acca Alert' advert. It featured such mouthwatering accumulator odds and possible profits that maybe, just maybe, there might be a way to wipe off all his debts in one fell swoop and still have enough funds to treat Ben. The only problem was that he had to win at least four bets in a row to secure the pot of gold at the end of the punters' rainbow. Oh, and find a significant amount of cash to make the initial stake worthwhile...

Thinking hard, he wandered over to the fridge and grabbed a cold beer. Feeling that some background music might relax him and help him to think more logically, Steve slotted a Paul Weller compilation into the CD player and pressed 'play'. He had forgotten that he had left the control turned right up when using headphones the night before, and the galloping rhythms of the Style Council's 'Walls Come Tumbling Down' came blasting out of the speakers at ear-splitting volume. He rushed to turn down the music, knowing that that his less than understanding neighbour needed no excuse to put her acid tongue to use. It was too late, of course, as the angry banging on the lounge wall indicated all too clearly.

But he couldn't help appreciating the ironic title of this particular track, and when it segued into 'Going Underground' he smiled wryly. The way things were shaping up for him at the moment, escaping into the bowels of the earth seemed a very good option indeed.

CHAPTER 7

Fridays were normally Ben's favourite days; he had the weekend to look forward to and as he was surprisingly well organised for an eleven-year-old, he made sure that school tasks were completed on time during the week so they wouldn't hang over him. Mikey, on the other hand, left everything till the last minute and usually messaged Ben in a blind panic.

Thinking of his best friend that Friday afternoon, Ben decided that the time had come to let him in on the secret he had been harbouring for the last few weeks. The plate-spinning pressure had now built to such an extent that a safety valve was necessary, and his pint-sized pal might be able to offer a fresh perspective. Once he'd calmed down, that is, because Ben knew that Mikey would be mega excited when he saw what the remote control could do and would immediately be fizzing with ideas.

Even just deciding to reveal his secret to his best friend

made Ben feel as if a weight had been lifted from his young shoulders. He messaged Mikey suggesting that they meet up by the swings close to his dad's flat on Saturday morning; that way he could pop in and see what progress had been made in terms of his promised 'sleepover space'. Knowing his dad's skill at putting things off, he suspected that a nudge in the right direction was likely to be required.

The ping on his phone signalled Mikey's reply. As well as confirming their meeting, however, the message contained a panicky plea for help with their latest Maths assignment. Ben got his school books out again and shouted down to his mum that he'd take Molly for her early evening walk when he'd 'solved Mikey's problems'. Not a bad play on words, he thought to himself as he turned to the pages on fractions.

* * *

Downstairs, Ben's mum was staring once more at the Jacks4Jills dating site. Her mood had improved since she had noticed that her profile had attracted interest from a certain 'Jazz Loving Geoff' and despite knowing next to nothing about this form of music, she was intrigued by his way with words and his other listed interests. 'Fine wine' – tick;

'Italian food and travel' – tick; 'Dog walking' – tick; 'Classic Hollywood Screwball Comedies' – tick.

The last of these she found particularly alluring as, when it came to films, Steve had always favoured the likes of 'Top Gun' and 'Die Hard', which in her opinion constituted macho nonsense you could watch with your brain removed. Give her the crackling dialogue and elegant fashion of 'Bringing Up Baby' or 'It Happened One Night' any time. In fact, a lockdown without Steve had given her the chance to binge-watch a succession of such classics and lose herself in the witty exchanges between Grant and Hepburn, Gable and Colbert and more. Ironically, the glamour of this black and white world made modern Britain seem colourless by comparison.

So, despite her frustrating experience with 'Guildford Guy', she felt curious enough to message back and suggest a trial meal at her favourite local Italian restaurant, as the 'Eat out to help out' scheme was now in full swing. This was somewhere she felt comfortable, and should the evening take a downward turn the friendly staff could easily arrange a taxi for her. The real stumbling block would be breaking the news to Benji, judging by his recent emotional outburst. Although he had made that joke about the 'eau de fox poo' perfume putting new men off, she knew that in his heart of hearts he was desperate for her to give his dad yet another chance. Perhaps it would be better to schedule the meal for a night when he was sleeping over at his flat – should Steve ever get his act together.

Having resolved on her plan of action and the detective work she needed to do, she felt the half finished bottle of Chardonnay calling to her and closed her laptop.

*   *   *

Ben, meanwhile, was now standing patiently at the entrance to the local park while Molly sniffed the clumps of weeds and caught up on the latest 'peemail'. He was about to pull her away when he caught sight of a striking and familiar face. Coasting along on her bicycle came Sarah Price, one of his classmates and the object of Mikey's affections, not to say worship. Her peaches and cream complexion, long blonde hair and cheeky smile made for a winning combination, and Mikey had been besotted with her ever since she had played Nancy in the school production of *Oliver*. The only Year 5 pupil to be cast in a major role, Sarah had delivered Nancy's stand-out number 'Whenever he needs me' with a maturity beyond her years, and Ben could still remember the ovation as the final note died away. Mesmerised, Mikey had watched from the wings, and Ben had had to drag him onto stage before he missed his cue and ruined the next scene, in Fagin's den.

Sarah drew to a halt and bent over to make a fuss of Molly.

'Who's a beautiful girl? Who's going to have a lovely run in the park then? Who's...'

'Hi, Sarah,' Ben interrupted, 'what have you been up to lately? Did you finish that fractions assignment on time?'

Sarah mimed a long yawn to signify her views on Mr Blenkinsop's latest task and then retrieved her mobile phone from her jeans pocket. She accessed her messages and thrust it in Ben's direction.

'Look at this!' she complained. 'Nathan Bolt's latest attempt to get me to say I'll go to the end of year disco with him, if we're allowed to have it, of course. He can't take a hint. He seems to think he's irresistible when I know just how revolting and cruel he can be. And he's even started calling me Sexy Sarah, which is just gross!'

Ben was quick to agree, part of him wondering what Mikey would make of Nathan's campaign. And then it struck him that using the remote to freeze time and embarrass Nathan in front of Sarah at the disco would make the perfect ending to the school year. All they had to do was engineer the ideal circumstances for maximum humiliation.

Switching his full attention back to his indignant classmate, Ben returned the mobile and pretended to be wiping dirty hands on his T shirt.

'Yuck. What a loser. At least I haven't had to look at his horrible face for ages thanks to the restrictions. But I'm due to meet up with Mikey tomorrow. Shall I tell him you said hello?'

Ben was keen to put a good word in for his love-struck companion and was racking his brains as to how to go about this when Sarah beat him to it.

'He's such a laugh, isn't he? I do hate the way Nathan picks on him because he's small and has to wear that horrible brace. If you ask me, when he's had a growth spurt and finished with the brace he'll make Nathan look like the one who's the nerd. Right, I need to go and buy a birthday card for my Nan. I'll see you around.'

And with that she was off, her blonde hair streaming behind her as she sped along the road which led to the local shops. Ben stood for a moment staring after her, imagining how Mikey would react to Sarah's comments. Spontaneous combustion wouldn't be out of the question, knowing his friend's passion for the Year 6 goddess.

At least he wouldn't have long to wait to witness this phenomenon. As he steered Molly away from a tempting pizza box, he grinned in anticipation of what Saturday might bring.

CHAPTER 8

Ben wasn't alone in looking forward to the weekend's possibilities, for his mum had continued to hit it off with 'Jazz Loving Geoff'. Last night she had almost felt like a teenager again on reading his latest flirtatious message. He had been badgering her to confirm a time and date for their Italian meal but she, meanwhile, was waiting for Ben to say when he would be staying over at his dad's. Knowing that he was going over there later that morning, she reminded him to persuade Steve to commit to a date.

'Honestly, Benji, I don't know how long one man needs to sort out a bedroom in a poky flat. I suppose he's too busy watching football or rearranging his precious record collection!'

'There's no rush, Mum,' Ben replied. He always felt rather defensive where his dad was concerned, although he didn't make it easy to fight his corner. Far from it, in fact.

'I'll ask him about it, I promise, but he's had other things on his mind what with his awful neighbour giving him a hard time and his sales figures being down. That's what he told me last time, anyway.'

Feeling less than sympathetic, his mum sighed and reached for a can of dog food. Molly's tail began to wag in anticipation and she jumped up so that she could get a better look at the glutinous mixture being spooned into her bowl.

'Mmm, what an intoxicating aroma - NOT!' Ben remarked. 'I was feeling hungry, but I think I'll wait till I'm round at Dad's with Mikey.'

'How's he doing? asked his mum. 'Still trying to beat you at your silly word games?'

'Well he's certainly trying,' Ben laughed. 'Very trying, in fact. But he just can't compete with the Maestro, the Viceroy of Vocabulary, the Doyen of Description, the...'

'The Master of Modesty?' Mum chuckled. 'Ok, off you go while your head can still fit through the door! And message me if your dad HAS got his act together and you are going to stay over.'

Having delivered her parting shots, she plonked Molly's breakfast down and switched on the coffee maker. She then shooed her son out of the kitchen and scrolled through the DAB radio channels until she located Jazz FM. The intense bass solo that greeted her was certainly a step out of her comfort zone, but she was determined to persevere. And, of course, it would give her something to talk about should Benji be staying over soon and her meal with Geoff arranged.

'It is a far, far better thing I do,' she murmured to herself ironically, channelling Charles Dickens as she poured a black coffee and settled down to expand her cultural horizons, all in the name of romance.

* * *

Twenty minutes later Ben was approaching his dad's new neighbourhood and Mikey's home turf. He was bouncing his football with each step that he took and looking forward to trying out a move or two on his friend when they indulged in their usual kickabout.

Spotting the swings they had chosen for their rendezvous, Ben took care crossing the road and checked the time. He was about five minutes ahead of schedule, which meant he wouldn't be seeing Mikey for at least a quarter of an hour, as he was always late for everything.

Plonking his football on the grass, Ben sat down on the middle of the three vacant swings and pushed off hard. He thrust his feet forward and settled into a rhythm that soon found him soaring high.

He hadn't bargained for what happened next. As he reached the highest point of the swing, the remote control slipped out of his back pocket and tumbled to the ground.

Mouthing a silent prayer, Ben watched as it struck the rubberised ground covering that surrounded the swings. Luckily, it bounced end over end rather than landing face down, and when he rushed to retrieve it he breathed a huge sigh of relief. The sturdy plastic case still appeared to be intact. He would have to try it out, though, if his carefully laid plans were to remain on track.

He was just considering his options when Mikey skateboarded into view.

'What have you got there, Ben? Why on earth are you lugging a prehistoric remote control around? And why does it say Star Wars on it? Maybe I should call you Obi Ben Kenobi!'

Before responding, Ben glanced around to check that the coast was still clear. It was unusually quiet for midday on a Saturday, so he decided to exploit the situation and check that the remote would still work its magic for him by giving his pal an impromptu demonstration.

* * *

'What the... what's going on? I can't see a thing!'

For a moment Ben was tempted to take a picture of his friend gesticulating wildly and doing his best to pull his hoodie from over his eyes. Instead, he chuckled and stepped forward to untie the tangled sleeves which had served as a temporary blindfold.

'Let there be light,' he said. 'You can calm down now. For a minute you were floundering around like a Spurs defender when a cross comes into the box!'

'But what happened? And how did my skateboard get up that tree?' Ben babbled. 'One moment I'm asking about the remote control and the next I'm wrapped up like a mummy.'

'And you'd better keep mum about what I'm about to tell you,' Ben advised, looking round again to check that nobody was in the immediate vicinity. 'Come over here to where I stowed your skateboard and all will be revealed.'

Once Ben had reached up to retrieve Mikey's board, the two boys sat down in the shade and Ben began to explain the voyage of discovery he had been on during the last few weeks. He explained how he had played the trick on Mikey by pausing time, removing his skateboard and dragging his hoodie over his head.

'And it wasn't easy doing all that while still keeping hold of the remote, I can tell you! I was going to tie your laces together so you fell straight over but I just couldn't manage it. I have to keep hold of it, you see, otherwise the functions don't work. And Pause and Mute are the only ones that do, for some reason.'

He had expected his pal to be feverishly excited about the prospects offered by the remote, so he hadn't bargained for the resentment Mikey now showed. Not letting him in on the secret had been an instinctive decision on Ben's part, one he still felt had been the right one, but Mikey was uncharacteristically bitter about not being trusted to share in trying out the time control tool as soon as Ben had discovered it.

'You could have told me, Ben. There I was worrying about Maths assignments when I could have been sharing in the fun and...'

'Well it's not been fun all the time, I can tell you,' Ben broke in indignantly. 'I can't remember when I was so stressed, to be honest. It doesn't always work the way you expect. Instead of sitting back and planning how to make Nathan wish he'd never been born, I seem to have ended up trying to bring my parents back together without them realising and hiding the remote away from both of them.'

He took a deep breath, calmed down and apologised for getting so wound up.

'Can I have a go? Mikey pleaded. 'Go on, can I?'

'Honestly, how old are you?' Ben replied. 'Four or something? Well I suppose it won't do any harm.'

Handing over his precious piece of plastic seemed like a very big step, but Ben couldn't begrudge his friend the opportunity to experience the magical sense of power that had transformed his life. He was also curious to see what it would be like to be on the receiving end, so to speak.

'Why don't you try muting me,' he advised Mikey, 'while I start to tell you what Sarah Price told me earlier.'

Mikey's eyes lit up at the mention of Sarah's name, but he pointed the remote at Ben nonetheless.

'You see, Mikey, I reckon she's got a soft spot for you because apparently she was really upset at some of the things Nathan Bolt said about you and...'

'It's not working,' protested Mikey. 'I pressed Mute when you said 'soft spot' but I can still hear you talking.'

'All right,' Ben replied, 'try Pause instead. That's the important one really.'

Mikey furrowed his brow and pointed the remote at his friend. As Ben could still see traffic crawling along the nearby road, and a family making for the swings, he didn't need to be a genius to work out that the remote was once again not responding to his friend's touch.

'Hand it over,' he said. 'You've got me worried now. Maybe it did get damaged after all.'

Mikey held out his hand reluctantly and Ben took back the device. Breathing deeply he pressed Pause, and immediately Mikey froze with his finger pointing over Ben's shoulder. It appeared that the remote still worked for him, thank goodness. But now a new problem loomed on the horizon in the shape – the very nasty shape – of Nathan Bolt, whom Mikey had spotted mid-stride about fifty metres away. Worse still, he was surrounded by his usual cronies or 'partners in slime' as Mikey liked to describe them. And it looked like they meant business...

CHAPTER 9

While Ben was agonising over how to deal with this latest crisis, Steve Wilson was endeavouring to make his flat look a little less like a bombsite.

The Hoover had had a rare outing and the kitchen recycling bin was now full of the empty crisp packets, crumpled cans and heavily annotated racing papers that told the story of his bachelor existence. To be honest, what passed for his spare bedroom was more suitable for one of the Seven Dwarfs than his rapidly growing son, although he had invested in a small sofa that doubled as a fold-out bed and above it he had pinned a large poster of that year's Tottenham squad. On the adjacent wall he had the cover of David Bowie's 'Aladdin Sane' mounted in a special frame.

'Cool,' he murmured, looking round the room. 'Not a bad sleepover space, if I say so myself. 'Ben's Den' is well and truly ready for action.'

Moving back into the open-plan lounge and kitchen

area, Steve thrust a sheaf of brown envelopes behind one of the sofa's corner cushions and switched the kettle on. He could see Mrs Snyde pottering about in her postage stamp garden and felt a brief twinge of guilt when he compared her immaculate lawn and borders with the scrubby patch of weeds he was responsible for. However, at least Ben could kick a ball about without worrying about damaging any flowers, he told himself. So really he shouldn't be losing any sleep over the state of the garden at all.

At peace with the world once more, Steve took his cup of tea over to the leather armchair where he spent a large proportion of each day. As he sank down it seemed to mould itself around him. When he balanced his cup on the arm rather precariously, he pictured his wife's outrage, her indignation that he could be so cavalier, or more accurately be so 'typically bone idle', as to ignore the nearby side table. At least he was spared that sort of lecture these days.

Reaching automatically for his mobile, he scrolled through the ever-increasing list of betting sites he had patronised and compared the various odds and offers. Despite their hollow promises of 'unrepeatable' offers, his heart wasn't in it somehow.

He knew that Ben was due to arrive shortly, so he wandered into the kitchen to assess his catering options.

As usual, his fridge was a vegetable-free zone and apart from two instant meals and some cans of Coke and lager, the shelves were largely empty.

Steve was just mulling over whether to make a quick visit to the corner shop when his front door was flung open and Ben burst in, closely followed by a gasping Mikey.

'Hey boys, where's the fire? I know you couldn't wait to see what I've done with the place, but you could have knocked!'

Steve had to wait for a reply, as both boys seemed too exhausted to explain and just stood panting by the window.

'Did we lose them?' Mikey asked his taller friend. 'I can't see over that blue Fiesta on the corner.'

Ben stood on tiptoe and peered through his Dad's dusty venetian blinds. The road looked deserted apart from a scrawny ginger tomcat performing its ablutions on the opposite pavement.

'I think so,' he said, ' but I'm going to keep an eye out for a few minutes more just in case.' Prising apart the dust-laden slats once again, Ben continued to scan the area like an undercover agent in one of his Dad's favourite spy movies.

Mikey breathed a sigh of relief and collapsed onto the sofa. 'Sorry about all the panic, Mr Wilson, it's just that we were about to have a set-to with Nathan Bolt and his fan club by the swings when Ben told me to run for my life!'

Still with half an eye on the road outside, Ben filled his dad in on the details of their close shave.

'You should have heard what he called Mikey, Dad. Nathan can be really cruel sometimes and the rest of his gang haven't got two brain cells to rub together so they just chant whatever he says. Mikey was so wound up he wanted to lash out but I knew we'd end up getting a real pasting so I tripped Nathan up and we just ran for it!'

'Well, despite what Bowie says, I suppose we can't all be heroes, just for one day,' Steve Wilson chuckled. 'When the odds are against you it makes sense to keep your powder dry.'

Hearing his dad use the word 'odds' suddenly made Ben feel really uncomfortable. He was all too aware of just why his parents were living apart, and when he moved a cushion before joining Mikey on the sofa, the telltale bundle of brown envelopes he discovered only served to confirm that his father hadn't yet learned his lesson.

'Dad,' he wailed. 'These are all bills. How could you! You promised me you'd sort yourself out.'

Ben's obvious distress cut Steve Wilson to the quick and his boyish features crumpled like the crisp packet he'd just picked up.

'I'm getting there, Ben, I really am. It's just that things are so flat at work that I've hardly earned any commission and...'

But he was now addressing an empty room, for Mikey had followed Ben into the garden, where the angry thud of ball against wall showed the depths of Ben's frustration.

Much as he loved his dad, he was finding it increasingly hard to make excuses for him. Earlier in the school year they had discussed the dangers of addiction in a PSHE lesson (personal, social and health), so he knew how hard it was to break any habit. Even so, surely splitting up the family had been enough of a warning to get a grip and break the cycle. He suddenly felt so frustrated that the thought of sleeping at his dad's for the first time didn't seem such an attractive option after all.

Heaving a heartfelt sigh, Ben picked up his football and challenged Mikey to a penalty shoot out. The space between two forlorn bushes by the fence made a reasonable goal, so Mikey got himself ready while Ben stood as far back as the narrow garden allowed and plonked the ball down. He only had room for a three-pace run-up, but he shot angrily and powerfully past Mikey's despairing dive and the ball ricocheted off the fence.

'Kane scores!' he yelled. 'And the mighty Spurs move ahead of Arsenal!'

'Not again,' Mikey protested. 'Why have I got to be Arsenal every time?'

Chuntering away to himself, he adjusted the ball and prepared to take his own shot. Knowing that Ben would have to guess which side to dive towards, he decided to be clever and chip it down the middle. But instead of embarrassing Ben with this skilful ploy, he only ended up embarrassing himself, because the ball sailed majestically into the air – and on into Mrs Snyde's garden.

'Mikey!' Ben gasped, stretching to peer over the fence. 'What are we going to do now? The ball's only gone and landed right in the middle of some rose bushes.'

Before his friend could reply, however, Mrs Snyde's back door was flung open and her bony frame stamped its way across to the flower bed. In a voice as sharp as the thorns that guarded her prize blooms, she addressed the two miscreants.

'This is one ball you will NOT be kicking again, I'm afraid.'

And with that she punctured it with the kitchen knife she had been using to cut a freshly baked ginger cake and took it over to her recycling bin. With a sour smile of satisfaction she dropped it inside and turned to give the boys a final dressing down.

But it was Ben who was able to have the last word in this instance. As Mrs Snyde turned, he instinctively thrust out his arm and pressed Pause on the remote control. She wasn't going to get away with puncturing his favourite ball, that was for sure.

CHAPTER 10

As suburbia froze around him, Ben assessed his options. It was the spicy smell of Mrs Snyde's ginger cake hanging in the air like the pigeons caught in mid flight that made up his mind for him. He hopped onto the tree stump at the foot of his Dad's garden and jumped from there onto his neighbour's immaculately tended lawn. He was careful to keep holding the remote control, of course, and as he passed Mrs Snyde by the recycling bin he screwed his features into the most ugly and threatening expression he could manage.

Moving swiftly on, he entered her kitchen, where the ginger cake sat cooling by the open window. To the right there was a spice rack mounted on the wall and on impulse Ben reached for the pot of cayenne pepper. It was a struggle, but he somehow managed to flip up the lid with his right hand while holding the remote control in his left. He then sprinkled the cayenne liberally over the cake and was delighted to see that it blended perfectly with the rust coloured surface of the sponge.

Not that he would ever admit it to his friends, even to Mikey, but he had always had a soft spot for the Spice Girls, and as he admired his handiwork he hummed the chorus of 'Spice Up Your Life' ironically to himself. Next, he carefully returned the cayenne to its home in the spice rack and skipped back into Mrs Snyde's garden. As he was about to pass his dad's sour-faced neighbour, he paused and looked her straight in the eye.

'Mmm,' he mused out loud, 'we've already got a Scary Spice so shall we call you Ugly Spice or Nasty Spice? It's a hard choice!'

He then attempted to clamber back over the fence, but as he reached the top the remote control slipped from his grasp and for one agonising moment it seemed sure to land on Mrs Snyde's side. Thankfully, it bounced up off Ben's knee and like a sharp-witted slip fielder he was able to shoot out a hand and grab it in mid air. There was no time to congratulate himself, however, for he heard an acidic shout of outrage as Mrs Snyde spotted him astride the fence.

'Get down from there this instant, you young hooligan. Haven't you done enough damage already?'

The screeching was loud enough even to prise Steve

Wilson away from Sky Sports and he came blinking into the sunshine to defend his son.

'Don't call my boy a hooligan, you old bat. What's he supposed to have done, anyway?'

'What did you call me? How dare you! No wonder you have raised a juvenile delinquent if that's typical of the language you use. You both need to learn the meaning of the word respect, if you ask me.'

'Well nobody did ask you, so put a sock in it and do us all a favour,' Steve retorted. He turned on his heel and ushered the boys into the kitchen, where Coke and crisps waited on the work surface.

Mrs Snyde had also retreated to her kitchen, where the thought of a slice of ginger cake and a strong cup of tea lowered her blood pressure somewhat. Or at least it did until she took her first bite...

* * *

Oblivious to the chaotic events unfolding at her husband's flat, Margaret Wilson was busy researching 'Top Jazz LPs' and 'Instrumental Icons' on her laptop. 'A Kind of Blue' by Miles Davis seemed as good a starting point as any, according to critics and bloggers, so she had accessed some

YouTube clips and been surprised that there was nothing to frighten the horses in Miles' mellifluous tones. In fact, she found the vibe he created far more to her taste than the majority of Steve's 'Dad Rock' and a distinct improvement on the punk groups he still played in order to cling onto his rebellious youth.

The white lie she had told Geoff about sharing his love of Jazz was hopefully going to pay dividends if he proved as attractive in the flesh as he seemed on line. She would need, though, to do some more homework before trusting herself to get into any sort of detailed conversation, so perhaps delaying the Italian meal for a week would be the sensible option. She could always say that Ben was ill or that Molly had once again eaten something inappropriate that necessitated an expensive trip to the vet and days of careful monitoring.

But even as she plotted her next move, she was reminded uncomfortably of all the times she had lectured Benji about the importance of telling the truth and not hiding things from each other. Steve's secret and disastrous betting sprees had made this mantra ever more significant for them both, yet here she was about to break her own code. No, perhaps this should be a turning point. It was time to be honest with her son about her on-line relationship.

As for revealing to Geoff that her knowledge of Jazz was on a par with her knowledge of the offside law, well, she would cross that bridge when she came to it.

* * *

Far from crossing any bridges, meanwhile, Ben and his dad seemed to be burning them where Mrs Snyde was concerned. It was hard for them to tell whether the scream that came from next door was one of anger or anguish. The furious hammering on the front door of the flat indicated that they would soon find out.

'Batten down the hatches,' Steve Wilson chuckled as he made his way across the lounge. 'Storm Snyde's about to hit us!'

He then paused to face the boys. 'Is there anything I need to know before I face the full force of the blast?'

Knowing that Mikey had done nothing to feel guilty about, Ben decided that he should protect him by slipping out of the back door while his dad was left to deal with the impending accusations and criticism. Indicating with a shrug that he was entirely in the dark about what had caused Mrs Snyde's latest outburst, he ushered Mikey through the kitchen and round the side of the flat. Luckily, her tirade covered up any noise they might have made and as they crept round the corner the last exchange the boys heard involved Mrs Snyde ranting about someone ruining her cake and Ben's dad retaliating by suggesting sarcastically that he should play 'Ashes to Ashes' to mark the sad occasion.

'Ben,' Mikey asked as they stopped outside his house a few minutes later, 'is there any way you might have used the remote control to get your own back on Mrs Snyde? She seemed in a right state.'

Ben looked down at his smaller friend and tapped the side of his nose. 'Ain't nuffink to see here, guv.'

Mikey grinned back. 'The Artful Dodger's got nothing on you, I reckon. I'll text you later if there's anything you want to own up to!'

Having said goodbye to his friend, Ben whistled 'Food Glorious Food' to himself as he made his way back to more familiar territory. He was sure that Mrs Snyde hadn't found her extra spicy ginger cake 'glorious', but she had deserved paying back for such a vindictive act. Destroying his football had been cruel and unnecessary in his book, so he didn't feel too guilty about his liberal use of her cayenne pepper.

He grinned as he imagined what her first mouthful must have tasted like and crossed the street in order to take a short cut through the park. And that was when he walked straight into a familiar face...

Nathan Bolt saw that Ben was on his own and that he was also unaware of the two gang members circling behind and cutting off any possible retreat. His features contorted into an ugly smirk.

'Well, Weedy Wilson, you won't be wriggling out of my

clutches this time. I think we should have a little chat over there behind the groundsman's hut.'

His two assistants grabbed an arm each and frogmarched Ben over to the shadows, where they flung him down onto an old pile of grass cuttings. As Ben landed in the fusty, foetid heap, the remote control slipped from his pocket and Nathan snatched it up in triumph.

'What have we got here then? What are you lugging this around for? Is it so you can play make believe games with your microscopic mate? Pathetic!'

'You're the pathetic one,' Ben retorted. 'Give it back. It belongs to my dad anyway.'

A cruel smirk spread across Nathan's face when he saw how desperate Ben was to retrieve the device.

'That loser. Is this heap of junk all he can afford now he's gambled all your money away?'

His cronies cackled with glee at this. The reasons behind the Wilsons' separation were obviously common knowledge among Ben's peers and parents at school, but until now the lockdown had spared him further humiliation.

Tears of shame and frustration pricked Ben's eyelids, and he leapt up and lunged at the bully. In the struggle that followed, the remote control fell to the ground and Ben heard it clang into a petrol can that stood by an ancient mower. Panicking at the thought of damaging or losing his prized possession, adrenalin coursed through him and he shoved Nathan violently, sending him sprawling against the side of the shed before landing in an ungainly heap with an outraged look on his face.

Ben scrabbled for the remote while Nathan's gang members were helping their gasping leader to his feet. He brushed the dirt and grass from its casing and was about to use it to freeze time and escape, but stopped and slipped it into his back pocket instead. If he used it now, the element of surprise would be lost before he and Mikey had even planned their disco comeuppance.

To his right an old cricket bat stood propped up against a cuttings bin. He grabbed it, brandished it like a sword and began to back away from his captors. Even in this risky situation, he couldn't help thinking he resembled a pirate or dashing musketeer in one of those old films his mum so enjoyed. Luckily the fact that Nathan was obviously badly winded bought him a few precious extra seconds – as well as a degree of satisfaction.

Emerging from the shadows, Ben breathed a huge sigh of relief as he spotted Sarah Price with some of the other Year 6 girls over by the swings. He ran flat out towards the bench where they sat giggling, yelling her name and waving the cricket bat. He knew Nathan wouldn't want to embarrass himself in front of Sarah by losing his cool or chasing to continue to pick on him, so he slowed as he approached the group.

'Look who's been dragged through a hedge backwards!' Sarah laughed as Ben slumped panting on the ground.

'And he smells like he's been sleeping under a hedge, too!' her friend Maisie added, wrinkling her nose in disgust.

'Very witty,' Ben replied. But as he proceeded to brush old grass clippings from his jeans, he had to admit that he reeked as Molly had after she had been found rolling in the compost heap at the bottom of their garden.

'Anyway,' Sarah continued, 'What's all the fuss about? I know I'm irresistible but you don't normally scream my name and sprint fifty yards just to get to speak to me! And I certainly don't want to play cricket.'

Ben looked suitably abashed for a moment and then decided that honesty was probably the best policy. 'Sorry, Sarah, but Nathan Bolt and his gang were about to...'

'Say no more,' she remarked. 'If you needed help to get away from HIS slimy clutches then I'm just glad I could be of assistance.'

'Yuck!' Maisie exclaimed. 'Just imagine being clutched by Nathan Bolt!'

The other girls joined in with retching noises and suitably disgusted expressions, and Ben couldn't help laughing too.

'Have you heard the latest, by the way?' Sarah asked Ben, pushing a stubborn strand of blonde hair behind her ear. 'The school's got the go-ahead to have the end of year disco and awards evening after all. It's going to be held next Wednesday.'

'Cool,' Ben replied, his mind racing. He and Mikey had better get their thinking caps on if Nathan was to be truly humiliated in style.

A scan of the area around the groundsman's shed revealed no further sign of his nemesis, so he assumed it would now be safe to make his way home. Nathan would no doubt be licking his wounds and using his frustration to plot further unpalatable acts. Well, let him. The remote control in Ben's pocket offered possibilities the bully could only dream of.

'Right,' Ben announced, jumping to his feet and brushing himself down. 'Sorry to ruin your day, everyone, but I need to head home.'

'Ruin our day?' Maisie chortled. 'In your dreams, Benji-boy!'

Maisie calling him that reminded Ben about his mother and her on-line forays into the dating scene. Wherever he turned at the moment it seemed that a fresh plan of campaign was needed, and he increasingly felt like a beleaguered Tottenham manager. For the time being, he just had to hope that things didn't go all 'Spursy' on him.

CHAPTER 12

Back at home, Margaret Wilson was checking her emails prior to messaging Jazz Loving Geoff, or 'JLG', as she now thought of him. There was an update from Ben's school informing parents that thanks to the recent relaxation in restrictions, they were hoping to go ahead with the end-of-year disco and awards evening after all.

As the event was scheduled for next Wednesday evening, she thought that this presented the ideal opportunity to meet JLG face to face. She could attend the awards part of the evening and see Ben receive his certificates and – dare she hope – a possible prize, then slip away once the disco was under way. After all, the last thing any eleven-year-old wanted was his mum hanging around and embarrassing him.

But first she would have to have the serious talk with him about 'moving on' in her life. She owed it to Ben to be honest with him, no matter how awkward things might get. She knew that his dreams of his parents getting back together were just that, dreams, but she couldn't just callously destroy them, no matter how appallingly Steve had let her down. Suddenly she was reminded of the Yeats poem she had studied way back in her dim and distant school days. 'Tread softly…' Yes, that would be her approach.

She was about to wander into the kitchen to see if she had the necessary ingredients to whip up a quick stir fry for supper when she heard Molly rush to the door. Her tail thumped against the skirting board as she heard Ben's familiar footsteps and then she jumped up to greet him as he crossed the threshold.

'Steady on, Molly,' Ben laughed. 'You don't need to lick every square inch of my face!'

But the Labrador had now moved on to sniffing and nuzzling Ben's jeans, intrigued by the new range of smells released by his ordeal in the groundsman's hut.

'Benji, what on earth have you been up to? Your jeans are all stained and your back pocket's hanging off.'

Margaret Wilson bent down for a closer inspection and saw that as well as the grass stains, there was an oily smear running down the left leg of her son's denims.

'If I didn't know better,' she said accusingly, 'I would have said you've been fighting with someone.'

Ben sighed, realising that there was little to be gained by

denying it. He explained about Nathan's jibes and how much they had hurt him and as he did so his Mum's expression softened. She knew that it took a lot for Ben to lose his temper. Once again she rued the day her husband had placed his first bet, and the disastrous chain reaction it had sparked.

'Well we shouldn't waste any time or energy on Nathan Bolt, that's for sure. He's a nasty piece of work you'll be well rid of when you start at the grammar school. Now hop upstairs and have a shower. Throw the jeans down and I'll see if I can work some magic on those stains later and re-attach the pocket. But we'll have one of your favourite stir fries first.'

Ben suddenly felt exhausted. Rather than 'hopping' upstairs, he dragged himself to his room, where he slumped on his bed after slipping out of his jeans. He reached up to slide the remote control behind the Stormtrooper helmet, then closed his eyes as the smell of chilli sauce drifted upstairs.

In next to no time he was dead to the world.

* * *

Half an hour later, Margaret Wilson could be found putting the finishing touches to her spicy stir fry, enjoying her second glass of Chardonnay and humming along to the warm tones of Chet Baker. The latter had proved to be an instant hit with her, and listening to his melodic trumpet and laid-back vocals was like slipping into a warm bath. Once again, she could thank the gods of the Internet for the recommendation. Soon she hoped to be able to impress JLG with her cool taste.

She pushed the sizzling pan to the side of the hob and wandered over to the foot of the stairs.

'Benji!' she shouted. 'Supper's ready. Come and get it while it's hot.'

She returned to the kitchen ready to plate up the meal, but as there was no indication of movement from above she decided to nip up and check that Ben had heard her. The door to his room was closed, so she tapped on it and made her way in. Ben was out for the count and snuffling snores came from his open mouth. She stood for a moment, wine glass still in hand, and as she watched him she felt a wave of maternal love and concern sweep over her. Her little boy was growing up fast, and he had already experienced more than his share of heartache in an increasingly uncertain world.

She was about to give him a gentle shake when her attention was drawn to the Stormtrooper helmet above his bed. It seemed to be drunkenly tilting to one side, so she reached across to straighten it. She tutted in frustration, for it kept swinging to one side and seemed rather heavy. In order to give it her full attention, she plonked her wine glass down on Ben's bedside table.

That was when her son's eyes opened. He stared up in horror at his mother. In a desperate, instinctive attempt to avert disaster, he deliberately sent his mother's wine glass flying and sprang out of bed. As the Chardonnay soaked into his duvet, his mother whirled round, and Ben gasped an apology. Secretly, of course, he was busy congratulating himself on his quick thinking and thanking his lucky stars that his Mum would not be enquiring why an old remote control was sitting inside his Star Wars memorabilia.

'Oh Benji,' she chided him, 'now I'll have to change your bed as well as seeing to your jeans. A woman's work is never done!'

Ben knew from her tone that she wasn't really annoyed with him, however, and looking at the wine glass on the floor and his damp duvet cover he rubbed his chin thoughtfully.

'Rather an UPSETTING scene, wouldn't you say, mother?'

She tousled his hair and suggested they sit down to the stir fry before it got cold.

'And I suppose, Benji,' she added as they made their way downstairs, ' some spilled Chardonnay is the nearest a Spurs supporter is ever going to get to a champagne celebration.'

'Ouch, Mum, kick a man while he's down, why don't you!' Ben protested. 'Your stir fry had better be extra good to make up for that!'

CHAPTER 13

Each credit card in Steve Wilson's wallet could tell a story, but not one of them bore re-reading. A new agreement entered into, a new limit reached, new debts and interest mounting up... each plot line the same, each ending depressing and sadly predictable.

His options weren't just limited now, they were virtually non-existent. The garage would never agree to another advance on his wages. He had reached his overdraft limit with the bank and he could paper his toilet walls with the final demands and threatening letters he had accumulated. Although he was tempted by the possibilities an 'Acca' offered, he simply couldn't scrape together enough money to make the initial bet the life-changing one he needed. He was also painfully aware that he had failed to give his wife anything towards Ben's upkeep for the last two months.

Perhaps the time had come for him to go round and be honest with Mags for once. Not that he would call her that, if he valued his own safety. She had accepted his pet name for her in those first rose-tinted romantic days, but as their relationship had soured she had bristled if he ever tried to revert to it. He only had himself to blame, of course, but just for a moment it brought a warm glow to his heart to be reminded of the spark that they had once shared and their early carefree days together.

Looking out of his kitchen window, Steve watched Mrs Snyde watering her pot plants and refilling her bird feeder. He wondered if his acidic neighbour had ever been romantically attached, whether she had been unlucky in love perhaps and that was what had made her so embittered. For all he knew, she could have been a catch in her younger days. But when she saw the squirrels arriving to pillage the bird feeder and her face become an angry, vengeful mask, he rather doubted it.

He turned away and reached into a cupboard for a tin of tuna. A baked potato to accompany this and his supper was sorted. Food was simply fuel as far as he was concerned and he couldn't understand the endless recipe supplements and restaurant reviews that filled the papers, particularly at the weekend. On the other hand, however, he supposed that most 'foodies' felt the same about the acres of newsprint devoted to sports that he devoured.

* * *

Stir fry consumed and Molly walked, Margaret Wilson was in her bedroom assessing outfit options for her date with JLG. Ben, meanwhile, was busy reading a book review which Mikey had sent as an attachment. The class had read Michelle Magorian's *Goodnight Mr Tom* earlier in the year and their English teacher had offered a prize for the best review; the winner was due to be revealed at the impending awards evening. Ben had dashed off a rather cursory effort as he had had other priorities in recent weeks, whereas Mikey had poured his heart and soul into the task. He had found the story particularly moving and, of course, Nathan Bolt had delighted in spotting the tear in his eye when Mr Johnson was reading the closing lines in class. He had teased Mikey mercilessly ever since, and this made the thought of using the remote control to get their own back particularly attractive.

'Wow!' Ben mouthed to himself as he finished reading Mikey's effort. He thought it was a brilliant piece of work, and one that even the notoriously hard-to-please Mr Johnson would have to reward. He had always known about Mikey's sensitive side but he hadn't realised his way with words could be so striking - on paper, at least.

He had just started texting his friend to that effect when

the door bell rang and Molly started barking furiously.

'Get that, Benji, would you?' his mum shouted. 'I'm just in the middle of trying something on.'

When Ben yanked open the front door the last person he expected to see was his dad.

'Hiya, buddy,' Steve Wilson said with an obvious note of relief in his voice. He had been steeling himself for a chilly welcome, so he was delighted to see Ben instead of his long-suffering wife.

'I know this is a surprise, but I really need to have a word with your Mum,' said Steve.

'Okay...' Ben replied doubtfully. 'I'm not sure you're her favourite person at the moment, though.'

'Well that's why I'm here,' Steve continued. ' It's about time I manned up and was honest with her.'

He knelt down to make a fuss of Molly, scratching behind her ears in the way he knew she loved. As she shivered in ecstasy, Ben scampered upstairs to tell his mum that his dad had turned up.

She was trying on various items of jewellery and he could see from her reflection in her dressing table mirror that his Dad would be in for a difficult time. Sighing heavily, she told him to invite his father in. Having decided it was time to be straight with her son, perhaps she should take this opportunity and fill Steve in on her burgeoning relationship, too. Of course, he was the one who had upset the family apple cart, so why should she be the one to feel guilty about starting over?

Hovering outside the door to the sitting room, Steve Wilson suddenly felt as if he was back at school and the Headmaster was waiting to read him the riot act. He pushed the door gingerly open and stepped in.

'What mess have you got yourself into this time, Steve?' she snapped. 'You don't normally show your face unless there's a major issue. And why haven't I had anything from you to help with looking after our son? Too busy throwing away what little you've got on some old nag?'

At this point Steve had to bite his tongue. The open goal presented by 'old nag' would have to be spurned, given his weak position. He decided to ignore the jibe and instead do his best to explain the dire straits he was in.

Normally he would have grinned at this point and used one of his favourite group's song titles to point out that he indeed had 'money for nothing'. But the look on his wife's face signalled that he'd better not fall back on juvenile puns.

'Look, Mag... Margaret, I haven't got the cash to pay my rent or utility bills, let alone find something extra for Ben. I might be evicted soon and...'

'Oh, so your son's needs don't count for anything, then,' she broke in bitterly. 'We'll just have to fend for ourselves as usual. Honestly, Steve, I could throttle you sometimes!'

'Honestly? Well I am trying to be honest for a change so you can get down off your high horse and just listen for a change.'

And with that the gloves were well and truly off. The slanging match that followed was enough to send Ben diving for the Stormtrooper mask next door in his bedroom. He hated it when his parents were like this. With his finger hovering over the Mute button, he crept back and pointed the remote control at the warring couple. Luckily for him they were too engrossed in the squabble to notice what he was doing.

Which meant that they also failed to register the panic on his face when he pressed the button – and nothing happened.

CHAPTER 14

Ben quickly retreated to his bedroom and pondered his next move. With his parents' raised voices only adding to his stress, he tried to calm down by taking deep breaths and thinking logically.

In normal circumstances when a household device started playing up, you just changed the batteries or consulted the instruction manual's 'Troubleshooting' section. These were hardly normal circumstances, though, and he had a horrible feeling that the magic was wearing off, so to speak, and whatever he tried might jinx things altogether.

Perhaps he should consult Mikey, who was far more technically minded and would appreciate being kept in the loop. Yes, Ben immediately felt more positive and started to message his friend. They needed to meet up anyway, as the Awards Evening and Disco were looming and they had yet to finalise their plans for 'Operation Maximum Humiliation'.

Ben could also explain in person just how blown away he had been by Mikey's review of 'Goodnight Mr Tom'.

A 'ping' from Ben's phone heralded an excited reply from Mikey. He had checked with his parents and said that as it was only 7.30pm, Ben could come over for an hour or so. With the argument still raging in his mum's room, Ben was desperate to get away, and he could see that Molly felt much the same, as she was cowering in her basket on the landing. He stowed the remote control in his Spurs backpack along with his favourite sweatshirt. He then waited for a lull in hostilities and popped his head round his mother's bedroom door.

'I can't stand this anymore. I'm going round to Mikey's for a bit.'

And without giving his parents the chance to respond, he galloped down the stairs and out through the kitchen to where his bike stood propped up against the garage wall.

* * *

'Well I hope you're pleased with yourself!' Margaret Wilson turned away from her husband and went back to sorting through her jewellery box. 'You turn up unannounced, you pick a fight and then you succeed in driving our son away.'

Steve held his hands out imploringly. 'Oh come off it, Mags, you've been listing my many failings for the last fifteen minutes. If anyone's been picking a fight, it's you! Anyway, what's with all the bling? You're not getting ready for a date, are you?'

Even as he posed the question, Steve realised that, in fact, this was just what was happening. Of course, he only had himself to blame if Mags was looking to establish a new relationship, but the stab of jealousy he felt showed how conflicted he was.

'Well, since you ask, Steve, that is just what I am doing,' Margaret announced, 'and please don't call me that. Did you expect me to lock myself away like a nun? I had been meaning to tell you about Geoff, but it's early days and I've got to consider Ben's feelings too.'

Steve was about to quiz her about this 'Geoff' when his attention was drawn to the jewelled brooch in the shape of a fish she had set aside as a possible choice but then rejected. He knew that Mags had inherited it from her late mother as both were Pisceans, and he also knew that it was worth a tidy sum. And just like that he suddenly he saw a way out of his troubles, a way of raising enough cash to make his 'Acca' a life changing wager.

Part of him felt ashamed to be even considering it, but he was in such a financial hole that his desperation trumped any morals he might once have had. All he knew was that this brooch could be his passport out of poverty – if he could find a way of getting hold of it...

And then he remembered that his wife was a creature of habit and that tomorrow she would be doing her weekly shop at Waitrose; she always went at lunchtime on a Sunday when the store was generally quiet. As he still had a house key somewhere at home, he could nip round to pocket the brooch while she was out. He knew that she usually dragged Ben along to help with the bags, so with any luck the coast would be clear.

Catching sight of himself in the dressing table mirror, he wondered for a moment what he had become, what new depths he was plumbing. Then he pulled himself together and tried to explain in a bit more detail just why he had failed to make any contribution to his wife's household expenses for the past two months.

As he did so, Margaret Wilson just let the words wash over her. She had heard the excuses so many times before and could hardly be bothered to listen. She had decided on the necklace she would wear and she began to gather up the remaining items of jewellery before popping them into the silver box that – ironically – Steve had given her on their tenth anniversary.

'Have you finished?' she enquired, turning round to face her husband. 'I can't be bothered to fight any more, so why don't you just go. If you haven't got the money then you haven't got it. I know who has though, it's those bloody betting sites you spend all your time on. It's pathetic, it really is.'

Steve had no answer to this. Shamefaced, he escaped across the landing, pausing to stroke Molly on his way. 'You still love me, girl, don't you?' he whispered.

The half-hearted tail wag he received only served to make him more depressed. But then he thought of the brooch and bent down to stroke Molly's velvet ear again.

'I'll be seeing you again tomorrow,' he continued, 'but don't tell anyone!'

* * *

Mikey's mother answered the door to Ben, and not for the first time he was struck by her size: tall and graceful, she bent over to give him a hug, her long hair trailing over him like the leaves of a weeping willow tree. Mikey had somehow inherited his father's genes when it came to height, for his dad was a short, stocky man who bounced around like a rubber ball. His mother, on the other hand, moved languidly and never seemed in a rush.

'Mikey's in the garden,' she informed him. 'Would you like some lemonade after your ride over?'

'That would be great. Thanks, Mrs Matthews.'

'All right then, I'll bring you both a glass. Do go through, dear.'

Ben picked his way past the ornaments and photo frames that seemed to occupy every shelf and table in the Matthews' small lounge and emerged into their modest garden. Mikey was perched on the low wall that protected the flower bed, his eyes glued to the latest edition of his favourite magazine about model railways. The layout he had developed with his father was his pride and joy and took up most of the spare bedroom.

'There he sits,' Ben said in typical David Attenborough style, ' the rarely spotted Wonderful Wee Writer of the Eastern District. Let us observe him in his natural habitat as he relaxes before penning another literary masterpiece...'

'Very funny, 'Mikey retorted. 'And less of the "wee" if you don't mind. If you want me to check out the remote then let's go up to my room where we'll get a bit more privacy.'

The two friends wandered back through the lounge, picking up the lemonade from Mikey's mum on the way. Once they were settled upstairs, Ben launched into a diatribe about his warring parents, while Mikey examined the remote control.

'I don't know what to make of this,' he remarked. 'It's ancient and it seems to be a sealed unit, so I don't want to wreck it by trying to look inside. We'll just have to hope you can get it to respond one or two more times so that Nathan gets what he deserves. And if it stops responding we'd better come up with a back-up plan.'

Ben had been thinking about exactly this on the ride over. Nathan was due to collect the Year 6 Project Prize (despite his father doing most of the work), and Ben began to explain to Mikey just how they could wreak revenge on the bully – even if the remote was playing up.

CHAPTER 15

'Show a leg, lazybones!' Margaret Wilson shouted up the stairs the following morning. 'I'd like to get to Waitrose sometime this century.'

'Ha ha, very funny,' Ben replied as he tucked in his shirt on the way downstairs. 'I don't see why you need me to come, anyway. You're not so ancient you can't manage a few bags of over-priced groceries!'

This long-running argument was played out late every Sunday morning, but Ben knew that resistance was futile. If he wanted his mum to get his favourite ice cream or snacks, then he had to put up with the heavy lifting. At least he could sneak some other treats into the trolley on the way round the store, and there was always the chance that he might run into some classmates and catch up up on the latest gossip.

Molly was used to the routine and knew that extra supplies of her gravy-rich dog food would soon be appearing. She trotted back down the hall with her favourite chew toy in her mouth as Ben's mum dragged him out of the door, then immediately headed for the sofa. This was usually strictly off limits, which made curling up in the jumble of cushions doubly pleasurable. Ben's mum pretended not to know that this happened each week, and as Molly was such a comfort to her she was prepared to put up with the inevitable hairs that found their way onto her clothes.

* * *

Ten minutes later, Steve Wilson emerged from his hiding place. He had been watching from the disused phone box on the corner, but had waited in case his wife had forgotten something and came back unexpectedly. Feeling that the coast was now clear, he let himself in through the front door and made a fuss of Molly, who had leaped from the sofa to greet him.

'Just like old times, eh girl?' he said quietly. 'Now let's see if I can lay my hands on some buried treasure.'

Molly followed him upstairs and stood panting in the bedroom doorway as he pulled open the bottom dressing table drawer. He had watched carefully as Mags had slid the silver jewellery box into its customary home, and now its contents were at his mercy. He felt relieved when he spotted the sparkling brooch, but also dirty and ashamed. Nevertheless, he forced himself to carry on and pocket the brooch before sliding the box back into its drawer.

As he straightened up he looked around at the familiar pictures on the walls, the pale blue summer dress hanging behind the door and the perfume bottles lined up on the mantelpiece. He picked one up, sprayed the citrus scent onto the back of his hand and was immediately transported to a hotel room on the Amalfi Coast where they had spent their honeymoon.

'You idiot,' he murmured to himself, his eyes suddenly welling up with tears. 'It's not just money you've lost.'

And with that he put the perfume bottle back down and made his way downstairs. Stopping only to make a final fuss of Molly, he escaped through the front door and locked it carefully behind him.

Now he just had to hope, as Yazz and the Plastic Population so memorably put it, that the only way was up...

*　*　*

'Oh look, isn't that Ben over there by the fish counter?' Sarah Price said, grabbing Maisie Williams' arm. The two girls were in Waitrose in the hope of finding a suitable box of chocolates to give to their netball coach. They had both come on in leaps and bounds thanks to Mrs Privett's patient instruction and they would certainly miss her when they moved on at the end of the school year.

'It certainly is,' Maisie giggled, 'let's see what he's been up to.' She had a soft spot for Ben and harboured hopes of a dance or two at the forthcoming disco.

The two girls weaved in and out of the shopping trolleys and ended up on either side of Ben, who was stifling a yawn as he watched his mum taking forever to pick her fillet of smoked haddock. Honestly, what difference did a few grams either way matter? It was only going to end up in flakes in a dish of kedgeree anyway.

'Hi, Ben,' Maisie trilled.

'Hi, Ben,' echoed Sarah.

Ben was delighted to see someone under pensionable age, and soon the three classmates were busy swapping notes and looking ahead to Wednesday's event. Margaret Wilson looked across from the fish counter and smiled to herself: what a relief it was to see her son looking happy for a change. Recently he seemed to have been so preoccupied for some reason.

She wandered over and tossed the sealed bag of fish into the trolley.

'That's almost it, I think. Why don't you stay with your friends, Benji, while I just look for a nice bottle of white to go with the Kedgeree.'

'Ooh, Benji is it?' Maisie cooed sarcastically as she watched Ben's mum beat a familiar path to the Wines and Spirits section. 'Suits you, if you ask me.'

'Well nobody did ask you, thank you.' Ben grunted in embarrassment. 'I hate it when she calls me that.'

'It could be worse,' laughed Sarah. 'My dad still calls me his "precious princess" sometimes. I just think most parents never want their offspring to grow up. It's like something out of Peter Pan!'

*　*　*

Two hours later, after three bags of groceries had been lugged from car to kitchen, Ben was on his way to the park with Molly. He was texting Mikey as he went and chewing a wine gum reflectively. With only three days to go before the Awards Evening, they really needed to fine-tune their plans for 'Operation Maximum Humiliation' and make the most of the idea Ben had hatched the night before.

'Stop pulling, Molly,' he sighed, 'I'll let you off the lead in a minute.' But even as he said that, the Labrador had escaped from his grasp and was bounding through the park gates towards a group of boys playing football. Ben thrust his phone in his pocket and chased after her, cursing his lack of attention and dreading what might happen. When he saw who made up the group, his worst fears were realised – the over-excited animal was heading straight for Nathan Bolt and his gruesome gang.

CHAPTER 16

'Molly, here girl!' Ben yelled as he pounded across the scrubby grass. Even as he shouted the words, however, he knew that it was hopeless, because the dog was obsessed with balls and her attention was completely focused on the black and white Adidas one that Nathan was about to launch goalwards.

'Get away, you stupid mutt!' Nathan protested as Molly nudged the ball to one side before pushing it along with her muzzle in a meandering doggy dribble. Ben was closing the gap, but he was still twenty yards away when the bully launched a vicious and frustrated kick at the excited animal. Molly let out a yelp of agony and limped to the side of the makeshift pitch, where she lay down and attempted to lick the back leg that had absorbed the full force of the kick.

'You brute!' Ben screamed as he knelt down to comfort her. 'You didn't need to do that, she was only playing.'

Nathan merely smirked as he tossed the ball to one of his acolytes. 'Don't blame me if you can't keep your dog under control. There've been some violent attacks around here recently and I didn't want to be another victim.'

Ben was incensed by this stage and spat out his response.

'What did you think she was? A Pitbull trained to attack? You know Molly's as soft as butter and yet you couldn't wait to inflict some pain, you sadist!'

'Oooh, such big words,' Nathan sneered sarcastically, flicking his greasy brown hair away from his eyes. 'Let's just hope she hasn't damaged my ball or you'll be buying me another. That's if you've got the cash and your Dad hasn't wasted it in the betting shop.'

His cronies giggled sycophantically and together they turned on their heels and left Ben consoling his whimpering pet. As he stroked her gently his mind was racing and he wondered if the remote control could be relied on to work its magic for one last time. If so, Nathan would be made to regret his cruelty in no uncertain terms.

* * *

Later that evening Ben had managed to control his anger and was consumed instead by a cold fury and a determination to exact revenge in the most humiliating way. It seemed that Molly had escaped serious injury and after allowing her a good half hour to recover, Ben had walked her slowly home. She had limped the whole way, however, attracting many a pat and sympathetic look en route and now lay curled up on the sofa with her head on his mum's lap. In the light of her ordeal, normal rules had been waived, and Margaret Wilson had a bag of dog treats by her side.

As he had never sent his original text, Ben had messaged Mikey to explain what had had happened and they were due to hold a council of war in an hour in a local café that specialised in delicious milk shakes. First, though, he meant to pop round to his dad's to remind him about the Awards Evening on Wednesday. Even if Ben wasn't in line for a prize, he would still receive a pen and leaving certificate, and it would mean a lot to have his father there. It would also show Nathan that he certainly wasn't ashamed of his dad, in spite of everything that had happened.

'I'm off now, Mum,' he said as he prepared to fetch his bike.

'Okay,' she replied. 'I'll stay here with the invalid and watch some mindless TV. By the way, if you really do want your father to come on Wednesday, tell him to dress appropriately for once. And don't lose track of time when you see Mikey, make sure you're back before it gets dark.'

Ben spent the ten-minute ride mulling over his schemes for Nathan. As he approached his dad's flat he thought he had two serviceable options, one which relied on the remote control and one which would be his back-up plan. Feeling pleased with himself, he leaned his bike carefully against his dad's side of the fence; he had quite enough to worry about without antagonising that sourpuss Mrs Snyde by invading her space.

He was about to knock on the door when he spotted his dad through the lounge window. He was standing there holding something up to the light. It sparkled as he did so and as Ben leaned in for a closer look his heart sank. He recognised the Pisces brooch that his mother sometimes wore on special occasions and he knew instinctively what this meant. His father must have taken it without her knowing in order to fund his gambling habit.

Waves of anger and frustration engulfed him and he strode over to bang his fist on the front door.

'I wasn't expecting to see you, buddy,' Steve Wilson remarked as he opened the door. David Bowie's "Fame" was playing in the background and he was wearing his favourite jeans and a white T shirt.

'How could you, Dad?' Ben wailed before the door had even been closed. 'How could you be so bloody stupid?'

'Language, Ben, language,' Steve Wilson tutted. 'What's got your knickers in a twist all of a sudden?'

'Don't try and make jokes, Dad,' Ben continued, near to tears by now. 'I saw you through the window with Mum's brooch. For God's sake, how did you get your hands on that?'

Steve was about to launch into a litany of self-serving, self-pitying excuses for what he had done when he took a long hard look at his son. Ben could not have been more upset, his face a crumpled mask of grief and disappointment. He suddenly realised how low he had sunk, how much his pursuit of the big pay-off had warped his judgement and sense of priorities.

He held out his hand, the brooch catching the light enticingly as he did so. 'Yeah, you're right. Your dad's no better than a common thief. Maybe you could slip this back into your mum's jewellery box before she notices it's missing. I just thought I had a way out, the means to solve all our problems in one go and...'

'You're the one with the problem,' Ben sobbed. 'Don't bring anyone else into this. I'll take it back home but I don't know whether I can face seeing you again and I certainly don't want you at the Awards Evening on Wednesday. You've probably forgotten about it anyway.'

And with that Ben stormed out, leaving Steve Wilson feeling that his guts had been ripped out and that his heart was as empty as his bank account.

CHAPTER 17

Ben messaged Mikey before cycling home, explaining that he had yet another family crisis to deal with and that they would have to meet up on Monday instead. He then tore back through the streets, hoping against hope that his mother wasn't once again trying out various combinations of clothes and jewellery. If she was, she could hardly fail to notice that her brooch was missing.

He skidded into his driveway and stowed his bike away in the garage. He then paused, panting, realising that he needed a plausible excuse for his sudden return home. Coming up with another white lie wouldn't be difficult, but how he wished his dad hadn't put him in that position.

Having decided that the unexpected arrival of one of Mikey's aunts sounded as good a reason as any, Ben let himself in through the kitchen. There was no sign of his mum, but the half-empty bottle of Valpolicella on the table revealed that she couldn't be far away. Worryingly, she wasn't in the lounge either, where Molly lay on the sofa looking guilty, but not guilty enough to give up her prime spot.

By now, Ben was fearing the worst and called upstairs.

'Mum, I'm back. Mikey had to cancel as one of his aunts turned up out of the blue and his Mum made him stay and entertain the old bat... I mean lady.'

'That's ok, Benji. Could you bring the wine bottle up since you're down there? And then you can tell me what you think of these earrings and this top.'

Ben felt a clammy sense of dread. If she was trying on jewellery, it would only be a matter of time before disaster struck and she became aware of the missing brooch. His only hope was that there was enough life left in the remote control for him to pause time and return it. Even as he considered this, however, he realised that it might well be at the expense of Nathan's longed-for humiliation. Was saving his dad's skin really more important than getting revenge on the bully who had tormented Mikey and kicked Molly? Of course it was, he decided. Family had to come first and if it was up to an eleven-year-old to sort out this mess, then he was the boy to do it.

Having delivered the wine to his mum, he tried to distract her by asking why she wasn't drinking her usual Chardonnay.

'Variety is the spice of life, or so they say, Benji. I know it's not January but I've made a resolution to try new things and start living for myself a bit. And that means moving on emotionally, too, so I'm going to be honest with you now.'

Ben gulped. He could see that she had enjoyed several glasses of the Italian red and he braced himself for what she might say next. At least it was stopping her from trying on more jewellery, though.

'I've met someone on line. Geoff, he's called, and we seem to have hit it off, so I've arranged to have a meal with him at Pomodoro on Wednesday evening. Now I know you miss your dad and you'd still like us to get back together, but I can't, I just can't face being let down and lied to again.'

Ben could see how bruised his mum's feelings were and that like him she had been collateral damage in the chaos caused by his dad's inveterate gambling. Tears pricked his eyelids as he went over and threw his arms round her.

'Wow, I must be honest with you more often!' she sniffed, close to tears herself. 'I haven't had many hugs from you recently.'

She dabbed her eyes and then turned back to the jewellery box.

'Now what did I do with that brooch?'

*   *   *

'Please, please work,' Ben begged as he retrieved the remote control from its hiding place two minutes later. He quickly crept back across the landing and peered round the door into his mother's bedroom, where she was rooting around in the upturned contents of the silver jewellery box. He mouthed a silent prayer, pointed the device and pressed Pause.

'Oh for goodness' sake,' Margaret Wilson muttered as she continued her search, utterly oblivious to her son's panic as he realised that the remote was once again playing up. 'Where are you, you stupid fish!'

And just like that, the remote finally responded to Ben's second attempt and he breathed a huge sigh of relief. Wasting no time, he hurried over and popped the brooch into the drawer which had held the box. That way it would look as if the sparkly fish had slipped out of the box and was therefore not part of the upturned tangle on the dressing table. Seeing himself in the mirror next to the frozen figure of his frustrated mother was disconcerting, but he squeezed past her and once back in the doorway pressed Pause again.

Nothing happened. His mum did not move.

It was then that he started to get really worried. He had never considered the possibility that time might get paused indefinitely and was aghast at what this might mean.

He forced himself to calm down and thought back to the problems he had faced when propping up the poster during his mum's zoom call. Putting the remote control down had led to time accidentally resuming, so perhaps he should try that.

He put the remote down on the carpet and held his breath. No, his mum was still frozen, her hand hovering over the rings and necklaces. The traffic outside wasn't moving and a pigeon was suspended mid-flight above the lamp post on the corner. Desperate by this stage, Ben picked up the remote again and pressed Pause.

Eureka! He saw his mum turn to look in the dressing table drawer and heard her exclamation of relief when she discovered the brooch. He could also feel his heart thumping, and knew there and then that it would be asking for trouble to rely on the device again. When it came to exacting revenge on Nathan, the back-up plan would have to do. The important thing was that he had pulled the family back from the brink of catastrophe and perhaps even set his dad on the road to recovering some self-respect.

Wandering back to his bedroom, he glanced up at the Stormtrooper mask and out of habit prepared to slip the remote control back into its hiding place. But instead he went downstairs, out through the kitchen, and lifted the lid of the recycling bin.

Dropping the remote into the pile of cardboard and bottles felt like removing a huge weight from his shoulders. His life might have been thrillingly transformed, but he could do without the pressure and the decision making, that was for sure. After all, he was at the end of Year 6, not Year 11.

CHAPTER 18

Monday morning found Steve Wilson on his way to the dealership. Headphones firmly clamped on, he was singing along to Bruce Springsteen and attracting strange looks from passers-by as they heard the lyrics to 'Born to Run' being belted out enthusiastically, if tunelessly.

Ironically, he had joined Ben in feeling that a weight had been lifted from his shoulders. He had felt so wretched and worthless after his son had stormed out that he had immediately used his laptop to investigate Gamblers Anonymous and also see what help Citizens Advice could offer about coping with debt. The latter's plan for prioritising payments had proved a godsend and he now knew that his rent and utilities should be top of the list. There was also a useful sample letter for contacting creditors, detailing particular personal circumstances and asking for time to put a repayment plan in place. So when he got back from work he was determined to draft an appropriately adapted attempt and then send copies to all those he owed money to. He had also made an appointment to meet an advisor face to face on Friday during his lunch hour.

Consulting the Gamblers Anonymous site had also provided comfort; he could see that he was by no means alone, and if a compulsive gambler was defined as 'a person whose gambling has caused growing and continuing problems in many departments of life' then that was him to a T. He was able to find out where meetings of fellow addicts were held in his area and although it was a daunting prospect, he had made a promise to himself to go along.

He was also determined to get back to what he was actually good at and sell some cars. The extra commission would be crucial in trying to make his first debt repayments, starting with his rent, if he didn't want a visit from the bailiffs...

*   *   *

Monday was also proving significant for Ben and Mikey. Ben had reconvened their milkshake summit and had confessed to his friend that he had disposed of the remote control. Mikey was horrified initially, but when Ben walked him through the events of the previous evening he began to properly appreciate the strain his friend had been under. The fact that the remote was no longer functioning reliably was the deciding factor, and Mikey quickly agreed that they had to have an alternative strategy for dealing with Nigel.

'I know it would have been great to pause time and put lipstick on him or dress him in a netball skirt, but I have had another thought,' Ben said after wiping the remnants of his strawberry milkshake from around his mouth. 'We know he's going to be presented with the project prize, thanks to all the input from his dad, so how about making sure nobody claps and there's just a stony silence when he's on the stage?'

'Or maybe we could get the rest of Year 6 to boo or hiss,' Mikey suggested, warming to Ben's idea.' Not that they'd need much encouragement after what he's done this year.'

Ben was wondering whether this might be going too far when the boys' meeting was hijacked by Sarah Price and Maisie Williams, who burst noisily into the café. They were giggling over something on Sarah's phone and whooped with delight when they saw Ben and Mikey at the corner table.

'Hiya handsome,' Maisie tittered as she slid into the seat next to Ben.'

'Handsome?' spluttered Sarah. 'Maybe you forgot to put your contact lenses in, Maisie!'

'Ouch!' Ben exclaimed. 'It's good to know who your friends are.'

'We're only messing with you,' Sarah said with a twinkle in her eye. 'Actually it's Mikey who's the handsome one, if you ask me.'

Mikey immediately turned beetroot red and squirmed self-consciously. He knew Sarah was way out of his league and that she wasn't really being serious, but even just sitting next to her was the stuff of dreams.

'Well,' Maisie said next, 'are you two going to buy us a milkshake or not? And what's the latest gossip?'

'Boys don't waste time gossiping,' Ben grinned as he got to his feet. 'Come on, Mikey, time to put your hand in your pocket.'

As the two boys went over to the counter they debated whether to let the girls in on their plans. Ben thought it a sensible move, especially if they wanted to get the rest of Year 6 on side. Amongst the girls, in particular, Sarah was definitely Queen Bee and her influence might be crucial. Mikey had been enjoying secretly plotting with his friend, but now that the remote control was out of the picture he had to admit that the girls' extra input might be welcome. Not to mention the additional time it would mean spending with Sarah...

So, bearing gifts in the shape of two chocolate shakes and some brownies, they returned to their table and explained their plans for humiliating Nathan. The girls chewed the gooey treats thoughtfully and when Ben had finished speaking Sarah clapped her hands appreciatively.

'That's a great idea, Ben! I always said you weren't just a pretty face! I reckon we go all out and after a few moments of total silence there should be a collective hiss. I know so many girls Nathan has teased this last couple of years and they will be desperate for a bit of payback.'

'That's right,' Maisie confirmed. 'What about Jenny Stewart, for a start. Nathan's made her life a misery just because she's had a few spots. And then there's Maxine Cooper. She is on the chubby side but Nathan and his gang are always chanting "Supermax" or "Maxiflab" when it's break in the playground.'

'I know,' Mikey said with feeling. 'Once he's got his hooks into you he never lets up. I bet the teachers have a good idea of what he's really like, but he's so sly he never gets spotted or overheard when he's making my - I mean pupils' - lives a misery.'

Sarah reached over to give his arm a consoling squeeze.

'Well now it's going to be Nathan who gets a taste of his own miserable medicine. And after Wednesday, if we're really lucky, we can wash our hands of him altogether.'

CHAPTER 19

Across town, Steve Wilson was giving a powder blue Mercedes coupé a final polish. On a sunny day like today the sleek SLK model would surely interest someone eager to treat themselves, and if they had any doubts about doing so, then he was just the man to dispel them. He would use all his charm to convince them that they would be getting a very special 'one off' deal and then use a test drive to further work his magic. Yes, the old one-two tactic would surely lead to a knock-out sale, he could feel it in his water.

Straightening up, he noticed a tired looking Mazda MX5 approaching and his interest was piqued by the elegant figure that emerged from the driver's seat. A blonde forty-something woman in tailored jeans and a pale pink T-shirt, she pushed her designer sunglasses to the top of her head and sauntered over.

'Can I help you, Madam?' he asked. 'If you're looking

for an upgrade then I have just the model for you now that summer has finally arrived. I'm Steve Wilson, by the way.'

'Laura, Laura Black,' was the cool response. 'And you can spare me the normal spiel, I know what I'm looking for and it might be that Mercedes, but you'll have to do a lot better than the price on the windscreen.'

Steve had always enjoyed the jousting that went on between salesman and customer and felt that here was a worthy opponent. Wearing his most charming smile, he suggested they go for a test drive and disappeared into the office to grab the keys. He paused for a moment before emerging and looking out through the window couldn't help but note that, like the coupé, Laura Black was small but perfectly formed. Going out for a drive on a sunny morning with an attractive blonde was hard work, but somebody had to do it, he laughed to himself.

As he opened the car door he asked if she was comfortable being called Laura or would she prefer Miss or Mrs Black or even Ms.

'Laura's fine with me,' she replied, 'and in case you're wondering, yes, I am married but I'm in the process of splitting up with my apology for a husband and to celebrate I have decided to treat myself to an upgrade.'

'So, as Cyndi Lauper put it, Girls Just Want To Have Fun?' Steve chuckled.

'Well it's a long time since I thought of myself as a girl,' Laura said ruefully, ' but that's about the gist of it. Anyway, I'm making a fresh start in life and hopefully this SLK will be the first step along the way. If we can strike a deal, that is.'

So somebody else was also trying to put the past behind them and turn a new page, Steve mused. Coincidence or not, he had a feeling that his luck might finally be changing. This opportunity had to be carefully managed. He started the engine and pressed the accelerator to let Laura drink in the throaty roar that followed. He then pulled away from the garage and headed for the bypass, where he would let her put the car through its paces.

* * *

At the very same time, Ben, Mikey and the girls were walking away from the café, having agreed on their plan of campaign. The boys would spread the word among their Year 6 peers that Nigel's award was to be greeted by a stony silence, then a collective hiss. Sarah and Maisie would do the same with the girls and then even if a few of the bully's cronies did applaud, the message would be clear.

They were in a determined but celebratory mood as they approached a busy crossroads and it didn't matter to Mikey that the sun had temporarily disappeared, as he was still basking in Sarah's radiant glow. He reached across to press the pedestrians' crossing button for her, but as he did so he did a double take and poked Ben in the ribs.

'Hey, isn't that your dad in that sports car waiting to turn right?'

Ben looked across the street and was struck by how happy and relaxed his father looked with his arm resting on the lowered driver's window and his sunglasses tucked into his thick sandy hair. He could hardly believe this was the heartbroken parent he had walked out on only forty-eight hours before, and he felt a pang of guilt that he had been so hard on his father. It was good to see him back at work in his natural habitat rather than poring over the racing papers or being glued to Sky Sports.

'Yup, that's my dad all right,' he confirmed. 'Hard at work, if you can call it that!'

Maisie giggled and whispered to Sarah that he looked pretty cool for an old guy. They then scampered across the road as the lights had changed and waved to the two boys from the other side.

'See you on Wednesday!' Sarah shouted. 'Oh, and don't

forget to ask Maisie for the first dance, Ben!'

Maisie screeched in mock embarrassment, but as the two girls trotted off she turned to give Ben a meaningful wink and Mikey promptly nudged his pal.

'She's got it bad, if you ask me.'

'Well nobody did ask you, so keep your rotten romantic rigmarole to yourself!'

'Nice alliteration, Romeo,' Mikey retorted and as they made their way back to his house they carried on teasing each other in their usual good-natured fashion.

CHAPTER 20

Had she been witness to this scene, then a wry smile would undoubtedly have found its way to Margaret Wilson's lips. Somehow all the stars seemed to be aligning in the family's romantic firmament, and she was feeling quite skittish herself as Wednesday dawned and her date with Geoff loomed large. The Awards Evening might be marking the end of Ben's Primary School experience, but where she was concerned, it also signalled the start of a new relationship.

Humming along to Ella Fitzgerald singing Gershwin's 'Summertime', she considered which outfit to wear and held up a flowery dress to gauge Molly's opinion. A steady thump from a wagging tail seemed the equivalent of a canine thumbs up, so she hung the garment against her full-length mirror and checked her phone. Geoff was obviously feeling a similar sense of excitement and anticipation, judging by the text she was looking at.

She smiled inwardly and was about to respond when she

paused. After all, she didn't want to appear over-keen or – perish the thought – desperate. So she slipped the phone into her back pocket and shouted out to Ben that she was going to take Molly for her morning walk.

Next door, curled up on his bed beneath his Tottenham wall calendar, Ben was also focused on his phone. He had been feeling increasingly guilty about his last angry words to his Dad and seeing him looking so relaxed at work yesterday had prompted a change of heart. He decided that he would let him come to the Awards Evening if he wanted and sent a message to that effect before retrieving his uniform from his wardrobe.

As he looked at the maroon sweatshirt with its fisherman logo, he felt a pang of regret that his time at St Peter's had come to an end. Yes, Nathan had made his life a misery at times; yes, some subjects had proved boring or hard to master; yes, he increasingly felt that he had outgrown the place. But the fact remained that he had so many precious memories to look back on, so many friendships and shared experiences to celebrate. Plays, outings and football matches; practical jokes, playground scrapes and even an embarrassing crush or two. His journey from shy seven-year-old to Year 6 Prefect had undoubtedly been life changing, even if much of it had seemed tedious routine at the time.

The ping from his phone brought Ben back to the present and he read his Dad's excited reply. Honestly, he thought to himself, it's as if he's the child and I'm the parent in this relationship!

*   *   *

What Ben didn't know was that Steve Wilson was messaging using a new phone. His exploration of the Gamblers Anonymous and Citizens Advice websites had flagged up the dangers posed by having access to the internet at the touch of a button. Reluctantly, therefore, he had visited one of the many local phone shops and swapped to the most basic of models, a 'dumb' phone that could only be used for calls and texts. 'Changes' had always been one of his favourite Bowie songs and he mouthed the stuttering chorus to himself as he folded the small device and popped it into his gilet pocket. He rather liked the Gareth Southgate look he was cultivating and just as the manager was changing the culture of the England football team, so he was improving the balance of his own life.

He stood up, stretched and looked at his watch. He'd better make tracks, as he was due at the garage before lunchtime and Laura Black was coming in to discuss a possible trade-in price for her Mazda. Steve had felt a genuine spark between them, and wondered if their relationship might continue after the sale went through. Suddenly life was full of possibilities.

He even managed to shock Mrs Snyde as he emerged from his flat by offering to carry her shopping in as she was struggling with two Tesco bags. Accepting in rather grudging fashion, she shot a beady glance of suspicion his way.

'What are you after, Mr Wilson? It's not like you to do something useful for a neighbour.'

Turning away from her front step, Steve gave a cheeky wink. 'What can I say? It's just that I've always had a weakness for a pretty face.'

And leaving Mrs Snyde gasping like a stranded fish, he jogged off down the path and headed off to the dealership.

CHAPTER 21

At six o'clock Margaret Wilson stood inspecting her son after doing her best to tame his stubbornly curly hair. A recent growth spurt meant that Ben's uniform was a little on the tight side, but all in all she thought he cut a fine figure.

'Now remember,' she said, 'even if you don't win any sort of prize, your father and I could not be more proud of you. If there's one good thing to have come out of our relationship, you're definitely it, Benji.'

Ben was about to protest about the use of his pet name, but he stopped when he saw his mother blinking back tears. Worrying about the strange remote control in recent weeks had distracted him from appreciating the problems she had faced and the effort she still put into looking after him. He reached forwards and gave her a big hug.

'Thanks, Mum, you're the best. Just make sure you're out of the way when the disco starts though!'

'You've nothing to worry about there,' she confirmed. 'I'm

due to be meeting Geoff at eight-thirty, so you'll be able to relax and bop away to your heart's content.'

'Bop?' spluttered Ben. 'This is the twenty-first century you know, Mum!'

'Less of your lip, young sir, or it will be the stocks for you,' his mother said, laughing. 'Now get off down to school and make me proud. Oh, and by the way, I've arranged with Mikey's mum for you to stay over as I don't know what time I'll be out till. I've put some bits and pieces in your Spurs bag with a bottle of wine as a thank you. Try not to drink it before you get there!'

'Very funny,' Ben said dryly. 'Seriously, though, fingers crossed Geoff turns out to be what you're looking for. And Dad will be around at school after all, so please don't start rowing if you do cross paths. That would be a real pain.'

'Don't worry, Benji, it's your night and nothing's going to spoil it,' Margaret Wilson said as she took both of his hands in hers. '

Looking into his mother's eyes, Ben hoped fervently that her words would indeed ring true.

* * *

'Settle down, years five and six,' Mrs Taggart warned the

buzzing rows of pupils. 'I know it's exciting for us to be allowed to be back together again but we have a lot to get through, and I would like to start by extending a very warm St Peter's welcome to your parents. I do hope you enjoyed the slideshow of the various activities that took place before lockdown.'

Dressed in a stylish lilac two-piece, the Scottish Head Teacher stood ramrod straight and exuded authority. Her staff sat behind her on the temporary stage at the end of the hall and a table bore the cups and books that were due to be presented. Like the pupils, however, her teachers knew that Jean Taggart's bark was worse than her bite and that she would always back them up in tricky situations.

The academic subjects came first, and amongst the English prizes there was Mikey's award for his outstanding review of 'Goodnight Mr Tom'. Together with Sarah and Maisie, Ben gave his friend an extra whoop of congratulation, but as he did so he spotted Nathan Bolt rubbing his eyes and pretending to cry like a baby. His cronies seemed to find this incredibly amusing, of course, and Ben thought back to how they had humiliated Mikey for getting so emotional at the end of the story. 'Just you wait,' he said to himself. 'Payback time is coming very, very soon.'

The 'Good Citizen' Prize came next and there was a

sense of keen anticipation as this was never such a clear-cut decision as the academic awards. Still seething over Nathan's mock tears, Ben wasn't paying a great deal of attention to Mrs Taggart until Sarah poked him in the ribs.

'I think she's talking about you,' she whispered.

'So, after consulting with my staff and canvassing opinion around the school, I have decided to award this prize to a young man who always makes time to help his peers and has set an excellent example throughout the year. Please step forward, Benjamin Wilson.'

'Well, you are a dab hand with time, I suppose,' Mikey muttered ironically as Ben made his way past.

Ben was aware of the applause as he made his way up onto the stage, but he could hardly believe what was happening. In a daze he shook hands with Mrs Taggart and received the small silver cup. He then turned and looked out over the sea of faces. He couldn't spot his mum, but there at the back of the hall stood his dad, a huge smile on his tanned face. Little did he know just how much 'time' Ben had devoted to him, of course...

'Our next award is the special Project Prize,' Mrs Taggart continued, her clipped Glaswegian tones echoing round the hall. 'This goes to Nathan Bolt for his amazingly detailed history of the local area.'

'Yeah, go Nathan!' one of the bully's supporters called out before shrinking under the Head Teacher's icy glare. But as Nathan made his way to the stage the few parental claps faded into a cold silence and then, after a few more seconds, a distinct hiss could be heard emerging from the rows of pupils.

Nathan's face was a picture as he slunk back to his seat and his outraged father proceeded to stamp angrily out of the hall, slamming the double doors behind him.

'Well,' Mrs Taggart said disapprovingly, 'that is most certainly NOT the way we do things at St Peter's. I don't know what's got into you all.'

The final presentations and leaving gifts were made in an awkward and uncomfortable atmosphere and the programme finished with the announcement of the following year's Head Boy and Head Girl. Mrs Taggart then swept out of the hall with a face like thunder but when he turned to his friends and saw the smiles on their faces, Ben knew that the first part of Operation Maximum Humiliation had been a resounding success, even without the remote control.

*   *   *

Ten minutes later Margaret Wilson was on her way to

Pomodoro and the hall had been transformed. The pupils had all carried chairs to be stacked round the walls and the teachers had strung up balloons and put coloured filters on the main lights. A Year 5 father who rather fancied himself, and who moonlighted as a mobile DJ, had suspended a glitter ball from the central roof strut and was now setting up his record decks.

Most of Year 6 had gravitated towards Sarah and Ben to celebrate the success of their condemnation of Nathan; amid the excited hum it was the voices of long-suffering victims like Maxine Cooper that seemed loudest. Maisie was busy teasing Ben about the first dance when she glanced over his shoulder and gasped.

'Would you believe it, he still hasn't got the message!'

Whirling round, Sarah saw Nathan and his gang smirking their way towards her. He pushed Mikey roughly aside and donned what he thought would be a winning smile.

'Ready for the first dance, beautiful?'

Instead of replying, Sarah looked him up and down then made a point of going round behind him and inspecting the polished floor.

'Sorry, Nathan, I was just checking for the trail of slime you've left. After all, I don't want to slip over when I'm dancing with Mikey.'

And with that she grabbed her startled partner and turned on her heel. Maisie cackled gleefully and dragged Ben along in her wake as the first chords of Pharrell Williams's 'Happy' filled the room.

Operation Maximum Humiliation had reached its successful conclusion.

CHAPTER 22

Steve Wilson, meanwhile, had been waiting in the playground and enjoying the evening sunshine almost as much as the message Laura Black had sent him. They had agreed on a price for the Mercedes coupe and she had even invited him to share a drive into the country at the weekend. At this rate he would soon be swapping his personal anthem from Bowie's 'Changes' to 'Golden Years', he thought smugly. He knew better than to count his chickens, though…

As the first dance track died away and the pupils applauded, he went over to the doorway to grab Ben's attention. Luckily, Sarah saw him waving and prised Ben away from Maisie's clutches.

'Well done, son,' Steve said as Ben blinked his way into what remained of the evening sunlight. 'That Good Citizen prize says a lot about you. I only wish I could say you were a chip off the old block. But, speaking of citizens, maybe you'll think better of me if I tell you I have been in touch with Citizens Advice and even Gamblers Anonymous.'

Ben had to admit he didn't know much about either organisation, but just hearing that his dad was finally trying to turn his life around filled him with a warm glow.

'So,' Steve continued, ' how about I treat you, Mikey and your lady friends to a celebratory pizza once the disco's over? I had a word with Mikey's mum earlier and she doesn't mind if you're a bit late getting back. It would really mean a lot to your old dad, and it would round off a great day.'

Still surfing a wave of euphoria, Ben held up a hand to high-five his father and said, 'It's a date, Dad. See you around nine. But let's pretend you didn't say 'lady friends' as it's really cringey!'

And with that Ben rejoined the fray, thrusting his way past the boys who had overdone the deodorant and the girls who looked just so much older and less self-conscious.

* * *

At nine o'clock Pomodoro was buzzing. The popular Italian restaurant's clientele was a mixture of parents waiting for the disco to finish, takeaway customers awaiting their orders and, of course, the odd romantic couple deep in conversation.

Margaret and Geoff were on the cusp of being in this last category. Romance was perhaps too strong a word to use at this stage, but they were certainly hitting it off, and Margaret was enjoying being with a man who acted his age and was more likely to read the front pages of a newspaper than turn immediately to the sport at the back. They had ended up ordering the same main course of Spaghetti Vongole and then had shared a feather light Tiramisu before downing a complimentary liqueur.

Margaret was just arguing that the Thirties rather than the Forties marked Hollywood's true heyday when she heard a familiar laugh and looked up to see Steve opening the door for the four children. Inside she was praying that her ex wouldn't ruin this evening as he had so many other occasions recently.

Ben rushed across to his mum's table and started telling her excitedly about Nathan's demise.

'Slow down, Ben, slow down,' she chided, 'you haven't even said hello to Geoff yet.'

Ben apologised and turned his attention to the tall man with sparse brown hair and a neatly trimmed beard. He couldn't have been more different from his dad and certainly seemed a lot older. What really grabbed his attention, however, was the smart polo shirt he was wearing with its iconic artillery logo. Surely his Mum wasn't dating a Gooner? As a Spurs fan he wasn't sure he could cope with the trauma.

Steve Wilson had also made the connection and thought to himself that if Mags was happy to start seeing a jazz-loving Arsenal supporter then he really had messed up. Still, as he introduced himself and assured Geoff that they would soon be 'out of his hair', he was thinking to himself, 'At least I still have some'.

Sarah, Mikey and Maisie had already chosen their pizzas, so when Steve ushered Ben across to the counter and ordered four Cokes and a beer, the two of them perused the menu.

He could sense how happy the youngsters were as the conversation bubbled away, and he would have given anything to capture this moment for ever. That was beyond even Ben's power by now, ironically, but when Sarah lifted up her drink and suggested a toast he felt a lump in his throat as Ben raised his can.

'Here's to no more Nathan,' his son laughed, 'and here's to fresh starts for all of us!'

Ben clinked his can against Steve's. 'And, most importantly, Dad, here's to no more gambling.'

His dad's reply could not have been more heartfelt, or more rueful.

'You can bet on it, son, you can bet on it!'